205

SOUL FLIGHT

Odyssey of a Psychologist

Marvin Rosen

ISBN: 978-1-312-33586- Printed in the United States of America.

Contents

Preface

In "Nightmare," Morris (Morrie) Schwartz, a

Philadelphia psychologist with roots in the Bronx, New York,

treats a criminal psychopath. The author refers to "Primal fear,"

a movie starring Richard Gere for inspiration about the theme of

the novel. In the present novel the hero has retired and moved

from the city to a far suburb in the country. He experiences a

number of bazaar happenings that challenge his neatly ordered

view of the universe. His training in empirical psychology is put

to a severe test and he learns his scientific discipline does not

have all the answers.

Curiously, the study of Kaballah, a Jewish mysticism

dating back to the Middle ages,

was also the theme of a Richard Gere film, "Bee season," from a

book by Myla Goldsberg. Kabbalah was also a central theme in

the 1992 movie thriller, A stranger among us, starring Melanie

Griffith. The author also acknowledges the influence of

psychologist-author Robert Lindner. His "Fifty minute hour," a collection of case studies and "Rebel without cause," a

hypnoanalysis of a criminal psychopath, was an inspiration that

clinical psychologists have something to contribute to literature.

Although the present author never met the first, he was graduate

student at The University of Pennsylvania at the same time as

Lindner's daughter. While"Nightmare was to some degree

autobiographical, "Soul flight" is pure fantasy.

1

The Aging Psychologist.

Morrie Schwartz, Ph.D., wistfully locked the door of his

psychology consulting office at the Presidential for the last time.

Rather than easing gracefully into retirement, Morrie in his

seventieth year, felt himself being dragged like a recalcitrant

child to the principal's office. It wasn't that he hadn't planned

for the golden years of his life. He had looked forward to

slowing down, traveling with Naomi, his wife of only five years,

perhaps doing some teaching, even writing a book. He had

shunned the many retirement communities in his area for a home

in Philadelphia's western suburbs where the half acre parcel was

sufficient to satisfy Naomi's craving for gardening. He ran

through the litany of advantages his new life would bring. Yet

there was the nagging doubt and uncertainty that he was really

ready to give up professional life. He let his lease at the

Presidential lapse and, while he still maintained his license,

terminated treatment with his fairly sizable patient load, referring several who continued to require help to his colleagues and long

time friend, Irv. . At the last year of the century he had burned

his bridges and needed to move on.

Morrie had changed over the years. His experience in

treating a deranged psychopath, who had attacked him in his

office, had mellowed him somewhat in his approach to his work.

The uncertainties of clinical diagnosis and treatment had shaken

his self-confidence. He no longer felt that he knew all the

answers. Empirical studies and research, which were an

important part of his training, had limitations. Morrie became

increasingly attracted to more subjective and even mystical

theoretical concepts. He felt himself drawn more closely to his

Jewish culture, his childhood experiences, his family values.

Metaphysical questions of mind and soul began to preoccupy his

thoughts. He delved into eastern philosophies when time

allowed. The loss of both of his parents led him to ponder about

the existence of an immaterial soul that somehow transcended

the organic self. While he had long ago rejected the outlandish and unproven claims of parapsychologists and the clever

deceptions of magicians like Urie Geller, he wondered whether

such things were perhaps possible. Even the technological

breakthroughs of geneticists and neuroscientists , identifying

chemical and organic linkages to psychological conditions he

had long attributed to learning and environment, did not provide

the answers he sought to the true meaning of life. Morrie

Schwartz, in his declining years, was entering the most

challenging and precarious phase of his life.

2

The Holy Grail: Search for the Human Mind

The object of Morrie's obsessing is the idea that there is a such a thing as "the mind," that it can be studied, and that psychology is the science that does that. It's not so simple.

What is the mind? Morrie mused. You can't see it or touch it. It doesn't have any physical matter. Is it just the brain, or is it something the brain does? Is it something that makes the brain do things? How could that work?   Psychology is usually defined as a body of knowledge about how people and animals behave. This is a very broad area since it includes behaviors that you can easily observe, such as learning to drive a car, as well as those that are hidden, such as thoughts and feelings. Psychology tries to understand the reasons why we behave as we do.

The most basic principle that Morrie accepted as gospel is the belief that behavior is lawful. That means that actions don't just happen. We do things for a reason, even though we may not be aware of that reason. The reasons we act as we do are not simple.

There are often many factors operating at the same time. It might involve changes in our nervous systems, our body chemistry, or even characteristics that we have inherited from our parents and grandparents. Other factors determining behavior have to do with what is going on around us-- what cues we are detecting from other people or events. Our behavior is also determined by our learning, past experience, memories, and even by events we don't easily recall.

Morrie was well acquainted with the history of science and the origins of psychology as a scientific discipline. Psychology as a separate science took a long time to happen. Until the end of the nineteenth century it did not exist at all, although the questions psychologists ask today have been thought about since ancient times. Psychology had two roots, philosophy and physiology.

Philosophy is body of thought and writings of great thinkers beginning with the ancient Greeks who lived 600-700 B.C. Philosophy provides the intellectual background for and antecedents of psychology. It encompasses efforts to understand an immaterial mind and how mind interacts with a material body. Whether they called it "spirit" or "soul," it has fascinated philosophers and religious thinkers for centuries If soul was different from the body, as the third century Greek philosopher Plato believed, then it created the possibility of a life after death. Plato believed that the soul was real-- more real than the world of the senses because it could contemplate universal truths such as beauty, goodness, and mathematical relationships. Plato's student Aristotle disagreed with his teacher, insisting that mind and body were united, that mind was a process of the body. Both Plato and Aristotle laid the groundwork for the 19th century application of scientific method to the study of human consciousness and behavior. Psychologists feel close ties to Aristotle because of his attempts to observe processes of human learning, memory, emotion, and judgment. He wrote vivid and readable descriptions of youth, old age, waking, sleeping, remembering, and differences between men and women.

Philosophers of the seventeenth and eighteenth centuries were still trying to answer the same questions. The great British, French and German thinkers tried to understand human nature as well as the morality of human behavior. Their ideas came from their own introspection-- what they thought was rational (reasonable), moral and ethical. They did not derive from experimentation and research. Yet, the scientific movement had already begun. Inventors were using laws of mechanics to build marvelous machines and philosophers were thinking of the human body as a machine. Renee Descartes understood that nervous and muscular reactions were stimulated by the senses such as vision and hearing. Reasoning and judgment, on the other hand, he felt were not mechanical but represented the soul. But how could the soul, which was without substance, control the brain? Since the brain was symmetrical, he believed that it must occur at some organ located in the middle of the brain. He identified this organ, where soul meets the body, as the pineal gland. No one accepts this belief as true today, but it illustrates how philosophers tried to solve problems by reasoning rather than by systematic observation and experimentation.

Another seventeenth century British philosopher laid the framework for psychology. John Locke (1632-1704) set out to understand the nature of human understanding. He attempted to define what it is possible to know and what is not possible and tried to answer this question by observations of human subjects and by inductive reasoning. It took him nineteen years to write his well known treatise, "Essay concerning human understanding. " Locke believed that the nature of human experience and thought was a result of the association of sensations that produce ideas. We come into the world with a mind that is a blank slate. The ideas we develop depend upon our experiences. Complex ideas are formed by the combination of simple ideas filtering through our sense organs. When we combine the sensations of redness, roundness, hardness, and sweet taste we develop the idea of an apple.

While psychology had its roots in philosophy, it was not until it was able to deal with the body that it could become a separate science. Physiology is the study of how the body works. Both Plato and Aristotle dismissed the brain as of minor importance in determining intelligence.

After Descartes, however, the brain began to receive increasing attention. The first anatomical studies were done in the early seventeenth century. A British physician, Thomas Willis published "Anatomy of the brain" with detailed illustrations. However, it took until the early 1800s for the significance of the brain to become fully appreciated. A German physician, Franz Josef Gall, played a leading role in popularizing the brain as the seat of higher mental functioning. Gall attempted to localize the various intellectual functions, such as memory and reasoning, as well as personality traits, such as benevolence and destructiveness, in specific parts of the brain. He believed that the shape of the skull in these areas was directly related to the shape of the underlying brain. This led to the pseudoscience of phrenology which became a nineteenth century craze. People went to phrenologists to read their personalities by feeling the bumps on their heads. This theory was later discredited when controlled experiments with animals were conducted in which various parts of the brain were removed and the results upon behavior evaluated.

When scientists began to focus primarily upon the subjective sensations and perceptions of people they became psychologists, not physiologists. This approach began with experiments designed to establish the relation between the physical characteristics of stimuli and the subjective awareness of small differences in these characteristics. This new discipline was called psychophysics and its leading proponents were Gustav Theodor Fechner and Ernst Heinrich Weber

The first psychological laboratory was established by Wilhelm Wundt in Leipzig, Germany in 1879. Wundt had been strongly influenced by Helmholtz, Fechner and Weber. He had

been Helmholtz's research assistant. Wundt studied many areas

of psychology by conducting experiments studying subjective

perceptions, associations, and reaction times. This was a new

direction that physiologists had not fully pursued before. Wundt

believed his procedures would lead to knowledge of how the

brain and nervous system worked; he was not interested in

practical applications. Psychology, he felt, should be pure

science. Wundt's work was so important that today he is

considered as the father of experimental psychology.

A major breakthrough in theory and methodology

resulted from the work of a Russian physiologist named Ivan

Pavlov. Until this time, many psychologists believed that

animals had conscious experiences and could make decisions to

control their behaviors. Around 1910, Pavlov had been using

dogs to study salivation as part of the digestive process. Dogs

naturally salivate when food is presented; it is a reflex and does

not have to be learned. As his research assistant climbed up the stairs to the laboratory to feed his dogs, Pavlov noticed that the dogs began to salivate before the meat had been presented! The dogs were anticipating the food, responding to the sound of the assistant's footsteps as if it was the food. This observation led to systematic experimentation in which two types of stimuli were presented together-- those that produced an unlearned response and those that initially did not.. When the previously neutral stimulus acquired the power to produce the unlearned response, Pavlov called the process a "conditioned reflex." In Pavlov's studies, a tone became the "conditioned stimulus" when it began to produce salivation without the presence of food. Often tones similar to that used as a conditioned stimulus also resulted in salivation. Pavlov called this process "generalization." The conditioned reflex generalized to the similar tone, even though it was never used in training.

Pavlov's observation of the dogs' salivation to a sound and his later research revolutionized thinking about the conscious experience of animals. Pavlov believed that the conditioning of an unlearned response explained not only how animals but also how humans learned complex behaviors and emotions.

Meanwhile, in Vienna, another revolution was taking place quite divorced from the main stream of experimental psychology. New ideas about hidden motivations for behavior led to a more dynamic conception of a divided personality with conscious and unconscious forces constantly in conflict with each other. Psychoanalytic theory and treatment developed in its own direction, quite apart from experimental psychology, creating two very different ways of exploring and understanding the mind.

Both traditional psychology and psychoanalytic thinking spread from Europe to the United States. Many American psychologists disagreed with Wundt. They felt it was important that psychology be help people deal with practical problems, like making teachers more effective. This idea resulted in many applications in schools, hospitals, clinics and businesses. It led to suggestions that parents could use in raising their children.

Research led to new ways of thinking and new theories of how people behave. Some psychologists believed most human behavior was a result of learning and conditioning. Others focused their investigations on social and environmental factors external to the individual

Morrie shook himself back to reality. He wasn't teaching freshman psychology any longer. His dilemma was his skepticism. How can the science of psychology, and its long historical development, be reconciled with the most basic human belief in an immaterial soul? How can science and religion be fused into a philosophical and empirical net? No less a thinker than Albert Einstein, probably the greatest thinker in modern history, rejected traditional concepts of god as a purposeful entity who rewards good works and punishes bad behavior. He saw God in the simple and elegant principle of nature, that he devoted his life to revealing. Morrie was not satisfied with that explanation. He wanted to know that their was a such a thing as a soul that transcended our material world, that linked us to a greater reality, that revealed our past and our future, and that was

not beyond our comprehension.

3

Altered States of Consciousness

Morrie's interest in states of consciousness originated as a preoccupation with dreams, his own and those of his patients. He found meaning, if not purpose, in his dreams and rejected the arguments of some researchers that dreams were merely noise generated by a sleeping brain. He absorbed as much of the psychological and psychiatric literature as he could, beginning with Freud's monumental "Interpretation of dreams." He found fertile ground in his own dream imagery for metaphors, condensation, symbolism and other dream work." He began to encourage his patients to make note of and report their dreams and it was useful in treatment. He experimented with the induction of lucid dreams in which the dreamer induces and manipulates his own dreams. Morrie rejected Freud's explanation of dreams as a camouflaging of threatening, forbidden libidinous impulses. Rather he believed dream imagery reflected the distortions of a sleeping but not inactive brain His dream about his daughter's landlord telling him to fix the pipes in her apartment, for example, appeared to signify his concern about her becoming "knocked up."

His interest in dreams led him to consider other states of consciousness, such as that occurring in hypnosis or under the influence of psychedelic drugs. He recalled the furor created by Harvard psychologist Timothy Leary who studied the effects of LSD. His use of drugs initially because of scientific interest went beyond acceptable professional and ethical limits in these pursuits. Morrie examined his own "hypnogogic states"—that transitional state between sleep and awakening, when free associations took over his thoughts. He was interested in the history of hypnosis, once labeled "animal magnetism" and thought to be similar to the force that moved iron filings between magnetic poles. He studied its use as a therapeutic technique by hypnoanalysts. He delved into eastern philosophies and the therapeutic use of meditation and saw linkages among these various approaches. His research and personal dream experiences led him to write a book explaining dreams and another dealing with hypnosis. He also was aware of the false ideas and misuse of these phenomena by misguided and naïve persons or outright charlatans.

Morrie acknowledged the existence of levels of conscious awareness, ranging from deep, dreamless sleep, to focused attention. Like Leary, he recognized the creative potential of states, where consciousness was less focused, such as in dreams, fantasy, reveries, hallucinations, and yes, drug-induced states. His reading and interest led him next to the consideration of paranormal phenomena, but that occurred only after some unusual experiences.

4

Morrie Takes a Vacation

Celebrating his new freedom, Morris and Naomi, in a sudden gesture of abandon, boarded a plane for Phoenix. With no special plans in mind they used the Hilton in Tempe a jumping off point, loaded their rented Taurus with hiking boots, cameras, binoculars, and compass and headed north along the mountain highway, avoiding Interstate 17, toward Sedona.

Ninety miles from Phoenix the road wound around the mountain, ascending to over 5,000 feet. The red rocks and scenic views provided Morrie with a feeling of awe and serenity that was spiritual in nature. As they approached the historic copper mining town of Jerome the road narrowed to one lane of hairpin turns. The town, perched precariously on the side of the mountain, looks as if it is about to tumble into the valley below. Indeed, some houses have actually been lost in that way. Morrie carefully pulled the rented Taurus into a slanted space, with the hood pointed out into space. Jerome, once a thriving community, serves today as an artist's colony and tourist attraction. The town was started as a mining camp in 1900 atop of Cleopatra Hill. It took the name of the original investor, a cousin of the mother of Winston Churchill. In its heyday it was the fourth largest city in the Arizona territory, with 15,000 souls. It was once considered to be "the wickedest town in the west" After the mines closed in 1953 the population dwindled to around 300 residents.

Morrie and his wife wandered around the town, window shopping, photographing the magnificent mountain views and sidewalk shops, gorging themselves on "the best burger in Arizona" at the Mile High Grill, and window shopping on Main Street. Morrie bought Naomi a collector's kaleidoscope at Nelly Bly's. They became intrigued by the history of Jerome and decided to stay the night so that they might visit the museum and take the evening ghost walk.

That night they stayed at the historic Jerome Grand Hotel, a Spanish Mission style structure with magnificent views of the Verde Valley. Morrie dreamed a maelstrom of images of early

Indian tribes who lived in the area two thousand years ago,--

Mexicans who had helped settle the area and afforded it a

Spanish influence, dust covered miners, whores from the Red

Light District, the "sliding jail," that had fallen to the next level

on the hill after a mine blast, and the fires in the 1890s that had

leveled several structures.

The following morning Morrie and Naomi headed for

Sedona.

5

A New Age

Psychologists are trained to be accepting of new ideas and the beliefs of other, while adhering to empirically established findings and therapeutic approaches. Psychology is a scientific discipline, deriving from both philosophy and experimental psychology. Throughout his professional career Morrie tried to adhere to the principles and ethical standards accepted by his profession. More than others in his field, he repeatedly questioned his effectiveness as a therapist, rehashed his strategies, and obsessed over his errors. He also maintained some degree of skepticism that empirical psychology did not have all the answers. Nevertheless, he was not prepared for what he encountered in Sedona.

Sometimes hailed as "the Mecca of the New Age, Sedona sports a psychic on almost every street corner. Morrie, who considered himself knowledgeable about personality, the thorny questions of the interactions of mind and body, and the

philosophic and psychological issues and risks of interfering in a
person's emotional life, was appalled by the preponderance of
untrained, self-proclaimed shamans, mediums, intuitives, and
healers. What galled him even more was the acceptance of these
prophets by the general populous of the city. Morrie was regaled
with every form of astrology, aura readings, card readings,
clairvoyance, energy healing, meditation, forecasting,
reflexology, compatibility testing, past life explorations, angel
channeling, flower essence, hypnotherapy, massage, yoga, tai
chi, ol gong, drumming, and healing gemstones. Psychics, for a
fee, will photograph your aura—an alleged ethereal energy that
surrounds the body. They quote freely from Edgar Cayce: "The
aura is the weathervane of the soul. It shows which way the
winds of destiny are blowing." Every psychic can take you to his
favorite "vortex," a specific point of intense energy that affects
living things. He will balance your aura, turn on your soul
vibrations, or guide your meditation to meet your angels.

Despite his skepticism, Morrie could not resist the impulse to visit one of these healers, although it was a daunting challenge to identify the most authentic from the outright charlatans. None of them had acceptable training credentials. Even if they had psychology degrees, Morrie believed they had sold out their discipline. In truth, he suspected they all promised more than they knew they could deliver. He assured himself that his interest in the experience would be limited to professional judgments and not any personal needs. Naomi, who was more spiritual than her spouse, was happy to go along with whatever he decided. Morrie used the Internet to choose a healer who advertised herself as a clairvoyant, clairaudient, and clairsentient, terms whose meaning he supposed he could guess. He decided to conceal his psychological training and degree. If asked he would describe himself as a recently retired businessman seeking spiritual enrichment.

Madame Fahita from Brazil advertised herself as a specialist in energy healing, intuitive counseling, and wellness training. In addition to private sessions, she provided classes and retreats to small groups. Morrie made an appointment and arrived on time. He introduced himself and his wife as Morrie and Naomi Schwartz from Philadelphia. Naomi would be allowed to observe his session but would not be the primary target of the initial assessment and soul reading. Morris agreed to the fee that purchased an hour of the medium's time.

"Do you have specific questions for me?"

"Before we begin I would like to know something about your training."

"Is that important to you?"

Answer a question with a question, Morrie thought to himself. Not unlike what he might do in treatment.

"It is. There are so many psychics in Sedona. How is one to choose wisely?"

"I was trained in Brazil by Roberto Rodrigez, whom you no doubt have not heard of, but who is well known in Brazil. I have known all my life that I have intuitive powers. I came to the United States and was drawn here by energy forces I could not explain. I have been practicing in Sedona for seven years and have treated hundreds of persons like yourself."

"Do you need me to give you some information about myself?"

"No, I have found it is better for me to read you first. I sense you will not be completely honest with me."

"What makes you say that?"

"Most people are well defended and seldom reveal more than superficialities."

"So have you already drawn any conclusions about me?"

"May I hold your hand?"

"Certainly, if that will help."

"You are skeptical about my skills. In fact, you have little faith in psychic healing. Youmust have learned to distrust at an early age. I wonder why you are really here."

"I am recently retired. I need to re-focus my life—to plan for my future, to achieve some balance and harmony."

"Those words are foreign to you. Yet, I sense you have some connection to healing.

Perhaps you are a physician…but no, it is not the physical self you treat. You, like me, are interested in the subjective self. Yet, there is a great contradiction in your life. You help people with personal problems, yet you are blocked emotionally. You have a need to accept a more spiritual orientation to life but you cling to the safest, most mundane ideas and approaches. You try to be objective. Yet you fear to explore the infinite, the most significant aspects of existence. You are not by design a religious person, yet there is a part of you that you keep submerged—a need for spiritual awakening."

"I was brought up in a Jewish family. I was bar mitzvah. I believe in God. Yet I see no need for rituals. I am a cultural Jew."

"For a therapist, you are remarkably closed to the forces of the universe. The principles of western psychology leave much unanswered."

"You believe I am a psychologist?"

"An extremely well trained and competent psychologist. But you could be much more. Shall I call you Dr. Schwartz?"

"I am a licensed, doctoral level clinical psychologist. But I am not the therapist here. Please call me Morrie."

"You have warm feelings about your parents and childhood. You were secure in your relationships and are still comfortable with people. Your mistrust is not in relating to people. It is much deeper. You cling to what is certain and are threatened by uncertainty. Your training would label you obsessive compulsive. Your meticulous approach to life wards off anxiety. You need to have things proven to you. Everything must be black and white. You were frightened by teachers in school You disliked Hebrew School and synagogue services. Not everything can be proven You need to let go, to expose yourself to the forces of nature that are all around you. There is much to be gained. Something has happened to you recently that punctured your self-confidence. Perhaps something with a patient."

"That's uncanny. Yes, I was attacked by a patient in my office. He stabbed me. I was hospitalized. I misjudged his aggressive nature. I continued to treat him."

"You needed to make things perfect, to ease your guilt."

"I had no guilt. I was doing my best."

"Yet you misdiagnosed him. Provoked his anger and allowed him to turn it on you. Perhaps it was what you really wanted."

"Perhaps you presume too much."

"Are you going to stab me now?"

Morrie, visibly shaken by the encounter, ended the reading and left the office. Driving back to their hotel, Naomi questioned him.

"Why did you become so upset? It was just getting interesting"

"I don't know. She overwhelmed me with her insights. She opened up issues I thought I had resolved in analysis years ago. Here it was a transference issue. I was identifying with my patient and experiencing his anger at me. Wow! I need to re-group."

"Are you going to see her again?"

"I don't know."

6

A Happening

They took the most direct route to Falstaff, where they would stay a day and go on to the Grand Canyon. Morrie was silent most of the way, rehashing his encounter with the psychic in his mind. Naomi, who had grown accustomed to his moods, respected his silence.

Falstaff's 7,000 foot elevation affords it cool summers and easy access to the Grand Canyon. Morrie registered them at the Hotel Flagstaff. They spent the day with obligatory sight seeing in the area but Morrie, still preoccupied, showed only halfhearted interest in the touring. They visited the Lowell Observatory, scrutinized the dinosaur collection at the Museum of Northern Arizona ands explored 700 year old cliff dwellings and archeological artifacts at the Walnut Canyon National Monument, established in 1915 by Woodrow Wilson. In spite of himself, Morrie worked up an appetite and by dinner time, at Black Bart's Steakhouse Saloon, he was back to his normal self.

He decided to put the psychic experience behind him, chalking it up to the unusual sensitivity of the medium and his own habit of revealing his feelings by body language. Whatever the source of her skills, he was sure they could be explained by purely natural phenomena. Early the next morning they drive the 81 miles to the South Rim of the canyon, finding their way to the Bright Angel Lodge, where they had arranged reservations and a one day guided hiking tour.

Morrie and Naomi were good walkers. They frequently hiked parts of the Appalachian Trail in Pennsylvania and had climbed to the peak of Mt. Manodnick in New Hampshire. But Morrie was not up to rugged climbing on this day. They picked the Bright Angel Trail to hike as it was the easiest trail in the canyon, descending 4.5 miles down to the Indian gardens and the Colorado River below. They had packed hiking boots and backpacks and arrived in sufficient time to meet the trail guide and a small group of tourists like themselves. Morrie found the hike to be less challenging than he anticipated and regretted not having arranged a longer and more difficult climb. Nevertheless,

he was able to enjoy the magnificent views and lose himself in

the splendor that the river had carved out over the centuries. The

following day they hiked on their own, managing to avoid

getting lost with the help of park maps and a compass. Morrie

felt the wonder of the vistas surrounding him, recalling

Einstein's conception of God embodied in the simplicity, yet

elegance of natural laws and phenomena. It was the closest he

had come to a religious experience in many years.

Morrie awoke at first light the third morning at the Park,

long before Naomi had stirred, left her a note, drove to Yavapoe

Point, 4,600 feet above the river to watch the sun rise. To the

east lay the Navajo Indian Reservation. He imagined himself an

Native American greeting the new day in prayer on this peak

He did some muscle stretching and then, seated, engaged in a

meditation procedure he had practiced as a young man . A

profound sense of peace consumed him, more intense than that

produced by any relaxation strategy he had ever attempted. Time seemed to disappear from his awareness. Had he been drinking or smoking pot he could have explained what transpired. What he later interpreted as an hallucinatory experience presented itself in the form of a Native American shaman in garb he identified as Navajo.

"Peace be with you, my son."

"And to you father."

"You have traveled a long way to be here."

"I climbed to the peak."

"You traveled in spirit, my son"

"I am confused."

"You need to allow your feelings to flow, like the river."

"I am frightened."

"You must not fear your own spirit. Allow your mind to expand and your feelings will free you."

Morrie felt a rush of emotion flooding him like the river. Tears flowed from his some inner well, long damned up but now disintegrating. He sobbed for many minutes as a young child.

And then the shaman was gone and Morrie returned to the
recesses from which he arrived.

He felt cleansed. The sun was still low on the horizon so little
time had actually elapsed. He made his way back to his car and
returned to the hotel.

7.

Retirement (Six Months Later)

Morrie awoke to the sound of a rooster crowing. The sun was barely up. He walked to the window and imbibed the bucolic scene before him. It was a lovely June morning. Rural Glenmoore, twenty miles northwest of Philadelphia was quite a culture shock for Morrie. Seeking to downsize his multilevel house, they found a more modest house with a first floor master suite, where he might avoid the retirement community and perhaps the nursing home, should either of them become incapacitated. On impulse they allowed a realtor to show them the house in the country. Morrie had given up private practice and had ended his consulting relationship with the school district. The house they found was perfect, but it sat on five fenced in acres of lawn and pasture. It had been a small horse farm-- miniscule compared with some of the surrounding farms. It was also a good 20 miles from center city Philadelphia. It was not what they were originally seeking but it was lovely. Naomi recalled her early experience with riding and it aroused in her an

intense desire to resume lessons and even, eventually, to own a

horse. Morrie, with a city background in the Bronx, was dubious

but, as always, eager to indulge his second wife in ways he had

neglected to do with his first.

In spite of himself, Morrie was making the adjustment.

Each morning he and Naomi walked a mile loop on McCleod's

Pond road for exercise, trying to improve their time. They

repeated the routine again in the evening. No longer engaged in

private practice, he volunteered at a program for autistic children.

They traveled whenever possible. Naomi continued to work as a

school psychologist at a local school. She was taking private

riding lessons once a week. Morrie started a novel, although it

was hard for him to abandon his academic style and give free

vent to his imagination.

***

Jeremy Craig walked the perimeter of his ten acre

farm. He checked the height of his corn crop, picked a ripe

tomato from the vine and munched it as he approached the pasture where his horses were grazing. Daisy and her colt approached the electrified fence as he approached and he held what was left of the fruit for the pony to eat from his hand. Jeremy, seventy years old, was still in reasonably good health. This wasn't one of those pristine gentleman farms, with manicured lawns and fancy stables, like those that now bordered Route 401. Jeremy and his son Josh had worked this plot of land since their parents died in the '80s. Jeremy's wife Sarah had passed away several years ago. Over the years they had received handsome offers to sell out to developers but they were firm in their resolve to maintain the family property and to make their living from it. In addition to working his spread, Jeremy and his son hired themselves out to do mowing, odd jobs, and renovations for their wealthier neighbors.

Morrie was browsing at the True Value Hardware store in Eagle for a toilet fixture. When he returned to his car he found it wouldn't start. As he repeatedly turned the ignition to no avail an elderly but trim looking man dressed in overalls and a

trucker's cap approached him.

"Goin' to wear down your battery that way. Let me take

a look."

The stranger returned to his Ford pickup truck and

returned with a battery tester. Without asking further permission

he attached the leads to Morrie's battery.

"Battery's got plenty of juice. Looks like it's your

alternator. I'll give you a lift down to the Sunoco. They'll come

out and take a look. Probably fix it right here. Hop in."

That started a relationship that rapidly grew warmer.

Morrie welcomed the company of the older man. Somehow he

related to his genuine earthiness. There was nothing pretentious

about Jeremy. His deeply hued, leathery features reflected years

of working his fields in the summer sun but his eyes had the

sparkle of a much younger man. Morrie saw him as the genuine

article, not like some of the neighboring country gentlemen

playing cowboy. Jeremy in turn was interested in the city

psychologist who had made his living talking to people. Before long Morrie was dropping in at the Split Rail Farm and even helping out with the chores. Naomi was delighted with Daisy and her pony Even Josh was happy for his father to have some company besides himself.

It was not until the following winter that Jeremy revealed more about himself than Morrie had anticipated. Naomi had invited Jeremy and his son to dinner. Josh excused himself early and drove the truck home. Morrie had offered to drive Jeremy later. Naomi retired early but the two men sat by the fire sipping brandy. The liquor loosened Jeremy's tongue and he asked Morrie if he had ever had any religious experiences. Morrie, who had recently joined the local synagogue, denied the existence of any significant spiritual needs.

"I'm not talking about formal religion. I .know you're Jewish but not too observant."

"Actually, I'm become more engaged than earlier in my life but I still am more a cultural Jew than anything else. I gain some sense of peace at services but I don't attend regularly"

"Have you ever had a sense of foreseeing the future?"

"Well, I've had déjà vu experiences. Everyone has. There is usually some logical explanation. I once went to a psychic…in Sedona. She told me some things about myself that don't see how she could have known. I dismissed it at the time. I also had a vision at that time in the Grand Canyon. Strange place, Arizona. All that beauty and grandeur. Does things to you. I've always felt there was more conscious awareness than psychology can explain."

"I've felt for some time that you had some special sensitivities."

"What do you mean?"

"I believe certain people have a certain awareness beyond their normal senses. People who see what others do not…who can receive energies around them…who can receive insights, knowledge that exist beyond our senses. I have always felt that I was such a person and I sense that you are as well."

"What gives you that impression?"

"There are times when you say something that I am about to say—as if I communicated it to you without words and without meaning to do so."

"Look Jeremy. I am a psychologist. I've always been somewhat intuitive. I read people well."

"Do you realize that you have been tracing something with you finger in the wet spot near your brandy snifter?"

"I always doodle when I'm at a lecture or just relaxed."

"You've traced some letters. Look at it."

"Looks like M-I C-A. Just random letters."

I never told you that Sarah and I had another son. Lost him to leukemia as a child."

"I'm sorry to hear that, Jeremy. It's not natural to lose a child."

"We never really got over it, Sarah and I. We had Josh two years after he died. Sometimes I feel his presence, watching over me."

"I understand."

"Not really. His name was Mica."

Morrie stared long and hard at his friend but did not respond. They drove the few miles back to the farm in silence.

8

Morrie's Crisis

Morrie's lifelong defensive structure was under assault. His training in objective science belied all that was happening to him recently. His need to partition the universe into what could be established empirically by objective research v. what was speculation, fantasy, unproven, or outright fraud was being challenged. A medium had revealed parts of his personality to which she had no reasonable or discernable access. He had managed to dismiss that experience as an aberration. He had seen a vision in some early morning dream-like state. He had more trouble integrating that experience into his well organized, highly structured mental apparatus but had put it on hold and preferred not to deal with it at present. But the doodling while talking with Jeremy was hard to ignore. It involved one of two phenomena —transmission of thoughts by Jeremy to him and communication with the dead through a process of automatic writing. Both of these possibilities lay outside the realm of reason. Granted, he had imbibed more bourbon than he was accustomed to handling. Yet, he was not drunk. He had driven Jeremy home with no difficulty. He had retained sufficient cognitive control to recognize that something extraordinary had occurred and to be disquieted by the event. No, it was not a lapse in what psychologists label "executive function" that had occurred. His ability to structure, evaluate, self-regulate had not been compromised. He felt a need to review what had been the psychological understanding that had evolved in his discipline.

A long standing concern dating back to the ancient philosophers had to do with the question as to whether there is such a thing as "the mind," that it can be studied, and measured. It's not so simple. What is the mind? You can't see it or touch it. It doesn't have any physical matter. Is it just the brain, or is it something that the brain does? Is it something that makes the brain do things? How could that work?

Psychology is usually defined as a body of knowledge about how people and animals behave. This is a very broad area since it includes behaviors that you can easily observe, such as learning to drive a car, as well as those that are hidden, such as thoughts and feelings. Psychology tries to understand the reasons why we behave as we do.

The most basic principle is the belief that behavior is determined and lawful. Actions don't just happen. We do things for a reason, even though we may not be aware of that reason. The reasons we act as we do are not simple. There are often many factors operating at the same time. It might involve changes in our nervous systems, our body chemistry, or even characteristics that we have inherited from our parents and grandparents. Other factors determining behavior have to do with what is going on around us-- what cues we are detecting from other people or events. Our behavior is also determined by our learning, past experience, memories, and even by events we don't easily recall.

While psychology had its roots in philosophy, it was not until it was able to deal with the body that it could become a separate science. Physiology is the study of how the body works. Both Plato and Aristotle dismissed the brain as of minor importance in determining intelligence. After Descartes, however, the brain began to receive increasing attention. The first anatomical studies were done in the early seventeenth century. However, it took until the early 1800s for the significance of the brain to become fully appreciated. A German physician, Franz Josef Gall, played a leading role in popularizing the brain as the seat of higher mental functioning. Gall attempted to localize the various intellectual functions, such as memory and reasoning, as well as personality traits, such as benevolence and destructiveness, in specific parts of the brain. He believed that the shape of the skull in these areas was directly related to the shape of the underlying brain. This led to the pseudoscience of phrenology which became a nineteenth century craze. People went to phrenologists to read their personalities by feeling the bumps on their heads. This theory was later discredited when controlled experiments with animals were conducted in which various parts of the brain were removed and the results upon behavior evaluated.

Obsessively, as if lecturing to the Psychology 1 students he once taught, Morrie reviewed the history of psychology in his mind—Helmholtz's studies of sensation and perception, Wundt's examination of the parameters of subjective experience, Pavlov's uncovering of the process of conditioning, Freud's clinical observations of neurotic patients and his concept of the Unconscious, the efforts of dozens of experimental and social psychologists to tease out the laws of learning, perception, memory, and social interactions and to formulate credible, experimentally validated theories of personality. This detailed mental review of the history of his discipline afforded Morrie some comfort. He came from a tradition of reasonable, careful, objective development of how humans perceived, thought, behaved. Science was self-correcting as new research findings

trashed or reformulated ideas that were no longer valid.

Morrie contemplated the history of nonscientific thought.

Somewhere, he mused, buried no so deep in the human psyche,

is a need to believe in the magical, the supernatural, the

miraculous. It is obvious in our myths and legends, our fairy

tales, our current literature, and our religious beliefs. The

shaman, the witch doctor, the magician in every culture and

throughout history surface and re-surface. Spells, incantations,

taboos, superstitions, magical potions, rituals, and prayers

become part of our conscious and unconscious. We cannot

escape their influence which their influences which bubble,

bubble, toil and trouble in our minds when we most need them.

In the film 2001, the obelisk appears before every breakthrough

in human progress. Dorothy searches out the Wizard in her quest

to return home to Kansas. We delight in reading Tolkien's

depiction of a magical pre-historic world. We avoid walking

under ladders. "Step on a crack, break your mother's back " The

Magician is accepted by Jungians as a pervasive archetype in our collective unconscious. These memories, some insist, lay buried in the deepest recesses of our right brain. There are no atheists in foxholes. UFOs continue to be spotted and we cling to the story of alien landings in Roswell, New Mexico, covered up by the Air Force. We continue to hear of poltergeists and Amityville horrors and extra-terrestrials. Morrie was always glad to debunk such concepts. But now, strange things were happening to him.

Morrie pondered these ideas for many days. It seemed to him that all the paranormal phenomena he had experienced – clairvoyance, visual and auditory hallucinations, and alleged communication with a dead son of his friend—if genuine, were based on the assumption that human consciousness can exist in the absent of brain activity. The clairvoyance presumed transmission of thoughts from one person to the other—a process rejected by Einstein and supported solely by questionable research and anecdotal evidence. Hallucinations are a primary symptom of schizophrenia, a thinking disorder. They are presumed to be a function of neurological or psychological processes of the person who is hallucinating. Morrie examined his own thinking and behavior and, other than the one incident on the mountain peak, could not accept that he was psychotic. If not mental illness then what? Drug- induced hallucinatory behavior? Morrie had never experimented with mind altering drugs. If not the doing of a disturbed psyche or poisoned nervous system, the only other alternative was some psychic energy floating around in the ether, devoid of a human nervous system. The automatic writing of the name Mica, a name Morrie was unfamiliar with, could somehow have been transmitted to him by Jeremy--again by unnatural processes—or truly represent the influence of a bodiless spirit communicating with him. Mentally deranged or not, Morrie concluded he needed help. He had not shared any of his bizarre experiences with Naomi. Now seemed like the right time.

9

Revealing

"What would you say if one of your patients presented you with the same story?"

Morrie had gone through each of his bizarre experiences. As he talked it brought to mind earlier incidents in his life. When his father became ill and could not be properly diagnosed in a West Palm Beach hospital he began logging his thoughts and feelings. One entry lamented "Dr. Radzinsky, where are you now?" The reference was to his family physician, growing up in The Bronx, who made house calls when he was ill. Later, at the family funeral plot where they were burying Sydney, he discovered that adjacent to his father's gravesite was that of Dr. David N. Rodzinsky. Another incident involved his mother's sister, who had died recently in Florida. She had no children but several nieces and nephews who gathered at her house for the funeral. 'Cousin Jane asked his sister, Loretta, how she had met her husband. Morrie chimed in that he had introduced them.

Murray was a dental student at Penn when Morrie was at graduate school. They lived at the same boarding house on Spruce Street and Morrie had brought Murray home to meet his sister. Loretta interjected at this point that she had a date that night when Morrie and Murray burst in unannounced. Morrie asked" "Who was it with, Arthur Vizelstone?"—the only boyfriend of Loretta's he could recall. It wasn't Arthur but cousin Jane burst out," I knew Arthur Vizelstone. Morrie was confused. Jane had grown up on Long Island, had never lived in the Bronx or Yonkers, Loretta's two addresses, and now lived and taught in Madison Wisconsin. "How could that be?" Morrie sputtered. "I was a visiting scholar at Yale. He was on the medical faculty. He died early. I was recipient of the Aurthur Vizelstone Award for Excellence." Both recollections are likely the kind of things that occur to everyone. We toss them off as strange coincidences. But are they, Morrie wondered?

Naomi listened with some degree of unease. She thought she knew her husband, whom she married as a widow several years before. Here was a side of him she had no idea existed.

She didn't know quite what to make of it.

10

Confronting the Unknown

The Split Rail Farm, a few miles from Morrie's new home, occupied a spot on Lyon's Run Road. Most of the parcels had turned over in the late '90s. The original farmhouses had been gutted, the fields turned into neatly manicured fenced-in pasture for the horses or pristine lawns. A few original farms, some in run down condition, now seemed misplaced among the larger, well kept estates. The Split Rail was still well maintained but it was clear that its days also were numbered.

Morrie arrived unannounced in his Nissan Pathfinder and saw Jeremy in the stall, grooming his horses. Daisy the mare stood by protectively as Morris brushed the new filly.

"Wondered where you'd been." Jeremy greeted him.

"I need to talk with you,"

"Sit yourself down on the fence. I'll be done here in a few minutes."

Jeremy went into to the house and returned with two bottles of beer. He steered Morrie toward two old rocking chairs on the porch, handed Morrie the open bottle and began.

"I could see you were upset the other night. Why are you so troubled?"

"Jeremy, you don't know me very well. I lead a well ordered, controlled, conservative, mostly uneventful life. I've always worked hard, made a reasonable living life. I've been true to my profession, ethical, never knowingly cheated any one. I believe that the universe is orderly… that it follows natural laws, including human behavior. Lately things have occurred to me that don't fit into that scheme. I find that disquieting, to say the least. Now you seem to be a part of that. Communication with the dead is something that falls outside the realm of anything reasonable. I know that people would like to believe that is possible—even rational, intelligent, thoughtful people— Sir Arthur Conan Doyle, Harry Houdini, for example. They have been exploited by charlatans and fakes. Now, at this time in my life, I am not ready to give up what I know to be true and accept some outrageous tomfoolery. I'm not that naïve. So Jeremy, how did you do it? Switch the pad I was doodling on? Hypnotize me in some way so that I believe I saw something that wasn't there? I've grown to like you Jeremy. Don't mess with my mind. I won't tolerate it."

"Morrie, you do me a disservice. I don't ask you to believe anything. I wouldn't want you to abandon your principles, your values, your most precious beliefs. You are you and I am me. Just let it go at that."

"You say that you have had communication with the dead and that I now have as well.Let's say for the moment that it was real. What other tricks do you do…read minds…predict the future…make things move without touching them?"

"It's not like that. I don't do parlor tricks."

"Then what is it? What do you do?"

"I don't *do* anything. It's more like a sixth sense. I just seem to be aware of things that others are oblivious of sensing."

"Messages just come to you."

"Yes, but not exactly messages. Just a feeling that something or someone is there, Sometimes I know who it is…like Mica…sometimes I don't."

"Do you see or hear things?"

"Not in the sense you mean. Not like an hallucination if that's what you're thinking."

"Then what?"

"I can tell if it is a reassurance or a threat or warning, or a direction to go if I'm undecided about something, or an acknowledgement that I made the right choice or a comforting gesture. Thats all I can say."

"But what does it all mean   Do you believe in ghosts?

"Again, not like you mean or like those depicted in movies. It is just a presence, an energy that's there. I believe I am like a receiver…an antenna. I've felt it all my life. I don't really know what the implications are. It's just there. I don't broadcast it. My wife knew about it and Josh. They accepted it. I thought you might have the same sense so I told you."

"Well, thanks for sharing…I guess. I don't know what it means either. If I have any more strange experiences I'll share them with you. In the meantime I need to think all of this through"

"Thinking is not going to do it, Morrie."

11.

The Age of Acquarius

And so it was that Morrie Schwartz, Ph.D., in the first year of his retirement, turned his attention to questions beyond the scope of his upbringing, his training, and his science. In so doing, he followed in the steps of illustrious others before him into the darkened mysteries of thought. Morrie Schwartz, long a cautious, risk-aversive, prudent, largely inhibited personae, in the twilight of his life, abandons his training and beliefs and, in uncharacteristic ways, finally breaks out.

Parapsychology, or Psi as it has been dubbed, is the study of paranormal (beyond normal) phenomena. It encompasses both mental and physical events. Extrasensory perception (ESP) refers to being aware of events by other than the normal five senses. Telepathy is being aware of another's thoughts or communicating thoughts without speech or other normal means of signaling. Other mental paranormal phenomena include precognition and premonitions, awareness of past life experiences, near death experiences, communication with the dead, and seeing apparitions. Physical phenomena include psychic healing, levitation, poltergeist activity, and psychokinesis, the power to move objects outside of physical reach.

Morrie knew that most claims of parapsychological events were unproven, based primarily upon anecdotal evidence or the work of tricksters and charlatans. Nevertheless, he acknowledged that, despite the lack of objective scientific evidence, some well known and respectable persons remained convinced. Harry Houdini, perhaps the greatest of stage magicians, clung to the belief, or at least the hope of communicating with his dead mother. He vowed to communicate with friends and relatives after his own death, but, despite the repeated efforts of a small group to establish contact, this was never achieved. To Morrie the most significant question was whether human consciousness exists independent of brain activity.

The pioneer of scientific efforts to study parapsychological events was Joseph Banks Rhine who had studied psychology at Harvard and later taught at Duke University. Rhine was impressed by a lecture by the renowned Sherlock Holmes author, Sir Arthur Conan Doyle purporting to provide scientific evidence of communication with the dead. Rhine established a laboratory at Duke to study paranormal events. His experiments used series of cards, asking subjects to identify the cards without seeing their face. He identified persons who were able to accomplish this task successfully above what might be expected by chance. Rhine's methods have been criticized as being statistically inaccurate and, in some cases, fraudulent. Most psychologists do not accept ESP research findings as valid and view the events as little more than parlor tricks. Morrie, on the other hand, was now willing to maintain a skeptical attitude

without dismissing the possibility that such events might eventually be substantiated..

Parapsychology advocates invoke the work of contemporary quantum physicists who study the behavior of subatomic particles. Their acceptance of probabilistic concepts date back to the German physicist Heisenberg, a contemporary of Einstein. Quantum theory leads to seemingly outrageous predictions that an object may exist in two places at one and that it is possible that a parallel universe exists composed of anti-matter. Quantum physics accepts a concept called "entanglement" to explain empirical findings of connects between subatomic particles separated by great distances. Measuring the properties of one, it is claimed, may affect another, even though they are light years apart. Some scientists have suggested that the entire universe may be entangled. Proponents of telepathy and ESP offer such data as evidence that paranormal influences are possible. Einstein criticized the probabilistic conception of the universe ("God doesn't play dice with the universe.") He abhorred the idea that reality is created by observers and rejected the claims of ESP adherents

12

Morrie's Dream

Morrie monitored his dreams more closely than most people. For over a year he recorded dreams assiduously and performed a content analysis. He was able to identify a small number of consistent themes, although the specific content of individual dreams always varied. He recognized that his everyday concerns and preoccupations appeared reliably. He learned to appreciate the metaphors that expressed these concerns and to identify symbols that signified anxiety and guilt. It was a disappointment that most of his dreams were boring. Any original thoughts of publishing them seemed foolish. He did use many of his own dreams in a book he published for secondary school student on sleep and dreaming. He abandoned his compulsive recording of dreams but would occasionally transcribe a dream he thought especially interesting for future use in writing or teaching.

I see myself as if watching a movie. I am four or five. I am sitting on the concrete sidewalk in front of the elementary school. I see the squares where children played boxball. The schoolyard below is guarded by a chain link fence. I am playing with a toy water pump. My mother is sitting with other ladies on camp chairs. There are other children in the group but I am playing by myself. Older boys are playing in the yard. It is summer. Soon I will start school. I approach my younger self. I offer the child a Hershey Kiss. My mother intervenes: "He can't have that. It will spoil his lunch." I am angry. I know he wants the candy.

Morrie associated to the dream. The image was similar to a home movie his father had taken with his 16mm camera. He had watched it many times growing up. The Hershey Kiss was not in the film. To him a Hershey kiss as a child signified warmth, love, security. At this transitional time in his life, was he seeking comfort and reassurance and longing for the safety of his childhood?

13

Morrie Breaks Out

It wasn't immediately obvious. He and Naomi still walked the country roads every day. Yet, Naomi was aware that something was wrong. She assumed he was still brooding over the events he had revealed to her, but Morrie was usually more resilient that he now was showing. He was definitely withdrawing from, her emotionally. He seemed less interested in his friends He seemed to be avoiding Jeremy. Each afternoon Morrie would seclude himself in the old barn that stood at the edge of their property. At first she thought he was fixing up an office for himself to write. But Morrie was never much of a do-it-yourself carpenter and he had few power tools. She was reluctant to pry into what he was doing. She didn't know how to handle it.

Morrie's pursuits were more arcane. Each afternoon he shuffled a deck of playing cards, then turned them face down and went through the deck, trying to predict the suit. He kept detailed records of the actual suit as it was revealed as well as his own prediction. After completing the deck he calculated his percent of correct predictions. After ten runs through the deck he compared his results to 25% chance accuracy, statistically determining the significance of any deviations. Repeatedly his results were slightly higher than chance--enough to tease him but not sufficiently high to become excited about It was likely that there were some subtle telltale marks of the back of the cards to which he was unwittingly responding. At least he was being honest in his investigation, he told himself, unlike Rhine, whose original findings may have been doctored by research assistants. Nevertheless, Morrie concluded, there was no definitive evidence that he possessed any clairvoyant skills in reading cards. Somehow he was comforted by this fact.

Next, he turned his attention to telepathy and precognition. Could he communicate with someone at a distance or read their thoughts? The most obvious target of these observations would be Naomi, but she must remain unaware that he was observing her.

Initially, he tested himself as a receiver of her thoughts. This would be difficult to test objectively. They knew each other too well and spent so much time together since he retired. He devised a scheme for classifying thoughts that he had relating to her. He omitted obvious things she might tell him about her daily chores, her work, her shopping excursions, her friends. He would count only thoughts that involved some unusual occurrence that he would not ordinarily be aware of knowing. He would write down any random thoughts about Naomi that met his criteria. He also recorded the time he had the thought. He chose an arbitrary time frame of 24 hours from having the thought. He then listened carefully to any thing she said that might relate to his documented thought. When he observed a "hit" he would record exactly what she had said and the time. He included any occurrence that corresponded to his thought, classifying these separately as accurate predictions. He maintained these observations for a month. It was during this time that Naomi was feeling most uncomfortable about her husband. Again, there was no evidence that he possessed any unusual powers of reading thoughts or predicting the future.

The next experiment also involved telepathy. Having shown he was not a "receiver" of thoughts from his wife, Morris wondered whether he could be a "sender." To test this possibility Morrie chose a strict criterion. He made a list of words chosen randomly from the dictionary. The target words needed to contain at least three syllables. They had to be relatively uncommon words, not words he believed Naomi ordinarily would use. Yet they also would not be so esoteric that she would be most unlikely to use. Morrie compiled a list of 100 such words including: :"catastrophe," "subservient," "supercilious," "flagrant," "monumental," and "derogatory." The list reflected a wide range of nouns, adjectives, adverbs using letters that reflected their general frequency of usage in the English language. Each day he chose three words from the list at random and concentrated on thinking those words and "projecting" them to Naomi. He recorded the words and the time he attempted to communicate them. He listed for the words during that day and until they both retired that night. Any form of the word would be accepted. After a month of performing these observations the frequency of successes was close to zero. So far, he had no evidence to confirm Jeremy's suspicion that he had any paranormal skills.

Morrie was beginning to feel silly spending so much time proving to himself what he already knew—that parapsychology, like phrenology, astrology, and reading tea leaves was a lot of bunk. Nevertheless he persisted. He would do what he had to do and then put the whole foolish notion to rest. He looked forward to moving on with his once orderly, sensible, usually productive life. Yet, if he felt ridiculous before, devising a test of psychokinesis was over the top.

Psychokinesis refers to the exercise of power over objects without actually touching them. Antoine Mesmer, a European healer in the 18th century, reportedly cured certain medical conditions by using magnets. He called his power "animal magnetism," assuming he could exert an influence by making passes with his hands or exposing the patient to a tree he had "magnetized." A scientific commission was convened to investigate his claims. It included Benjamin Franklyn, then American ambassador to France, as well as the inventor of the guillotine, and the chemist who isolated oxygen. The commission concluded that healing effects sometimes occurred but attributed healing to suggestion, not magnetism. The contemporary magician Uri Geller convinces observers that he can bend forks at a distance. While most magicians acknowledge their tricks are merely clever illusions, Geller insists his powers are genuine. He has been discredited many times but continues to convince people he can perform psychokinesis.

Carefully, Morrie traced the outline of a fork on a sheet on paper. He adjusted the utensil to ensure it was within the pencil outline. Moving back several feet from the table, he concentrated his thoughts with as much

effort as he could generate. He visualized the fork bending at both ends to

form a V shape. He moved his hands as if bending a heavy object, much as

a bowler gestures the ball toward the appropriate pin as it rolls down the

alley. Again and again he repeated the exercise, continuing for 15 minutes

without a break. If there was any psychic energy emanating from his

thoughts surely it would impinge upon the inert fork, accumulate at the tips

and exert sufficient pressure to form the V. Tiring, he approached the table

and carefully inspected the position of the fork. The fork continued to rest

securely in place as he had positioned it. Geller used some ingenious

method to make it appear that utensils moved, Morrie reassured himself; it

was not psychokinesis.

Morrie pondered the implications of his experiments. As

much as possible he tried to use objective statistical inference in

reaching his conclusions. Statistical reasoning is based upon

probabilities. There is no certainty about proving or disproving an

hypothesis. However, if the likelihood of a certain effect being

real is so small that it might occur only one time in 100 or less, and the event occurs, it is reasonable to assume that the effect is real. Experimental design generally uses treatment and control groups. Treatment groups are exposed to a treatment condition reflecting the hypothesis. Control groups are selected to match the treatment group as closely as possible, except for the critical condition. A dependent variable, which reflects the possible effects of the condition, is measured for both groups. The conclusion that there is no difference between the treatment and control group after the intervention is called the null hypothesis. The null hypothesis can never be proven. Small differences may exist but measurement wasn't sensitive enough to detect them. However, if differences are found, sufficiently large to probably not be due to chance, the null hypothesis is rejected. Errors may occur but their likelihood cam be estimated. If a scientists rejects a null hypothesis when it is really true (there is no true difference in the groups after the intervention) it is called a Type 1 error. If there really is a difference and it is not detected, it is called a Type 2 error. It is often the case that scientists are testing some favorite theory and are actually motivated to find a difference. If, unwittingly, they build a bias into their measurement, they are more likely to commit a Type 1 error. Morrie realized, on the other hand, that he really didn't want to prove himself to be psychic. He, therefore, would be more likely to commit a Type 2 error. That said, Morrie let himself off the hook. He had been faithful to good experimental design to the best of his ability. After all, it had been decades since he had actively engaged in research. . He had not disproved the assumptions of parapsychology with only one subject, himself, but he was the one person of most interest.. Let the parapsychologists prove their own theory. He could go back to being normal and live his own life.

14

Return to Normalcy

Rabbi Solomon Hershman convened the meeting

of the Temple Israel Men's Club. He introduced the

guest speaker, Dr. Morris Schwartz, Clinical

Psychologist, who would provide a lecture titled, "Stress

management in the new millennium." Morrie started his

talk by mentioning that, despite all the hoopla, 2000 was

really not the first year of the new millenium but the last

year of the 20th century. He joked that all the stress

generated by the media this past January, was not only

misguided but also premature.

Sol Hershman, age 35, grew up in Brooklyn, New

York. His parents were orthodox Jews, adhering strictly

to the Talmudic laws and tradition. As a teenager Sol had

rebelled against the rigidity of rules for keeping a kosher

kitchen, fasting on Yom Kipor and keeping the Sabbath.

However, Sol decided to take a year off between his

junior and senior year at college to live on a kibbutz in Israel, near the Lebanese border. His exposure to rigors of living in a danger zone, not far from the no-man's land maintained by the U.N., aroused a sense of Jewish identity that he did not know existed. When he returned to college the following September he became immersed in his religion. He maintained a relationship with many of he young Zionists with whom he had lived and worked. After graduation he enrolled at the Union Theological Seminary for rabbinical studies. After receiving his degree he accepted a position at a new synagogue in the small town of Eagle, Pennsylvania. Temple Israel was not the orthodox synagogue attended by his parents, but a conservative Temple. Sol married Rebecca, one of his congregants. At the time Morrie gave his talk, the Rabbi and his wife had a two year old child, Rachel.

After leaving the synagogue Morris reflected on his experience. He was surprised at his feelings of comfort within the Temple. It brought back images of his childhood experiences at the orthodox "schul" attended by his father. Women were segregated in a special section of the synagogue and did not participate in the service. His preparation for bar mitzvah was harsh, requiring the same diligence of study and homework demanded at the public school. He was intimidated at Saturday services and being called to read his "haftora" at his bar mitzvah was daunting. After leaving home he avoided services except for weddings and bar mitzvahs. He enrolled his children in a reform synagogue to learn a little of their heritage, but did not require them to become bas mitzvah. Had he borne sons, rather than daughters, it probably would have been a different story. Yet on this day Morrie was moved by the warmth and congeniality extended to him at Temple Israel and made a mental note to attend a Saturday morning service in the near future. It was a resolve that would take several months before being fulfilled.

Morrie resumed his new life in the country. He and Naomi continued their daily walking regimen. Morris paid a lawn service to mow and trim his property but planted trees and shrubs in the fall and maintained a compost pile for the flower beds. He was eating healthier under Naomi's prodding and the daily exercise kept him trim. The bizarre events of the past few months were fading in significance to him.

15

Out-of-body or Out-of-mind

(One year later)

Morrie had accepted a temporary teaching position at a community college. He was allowed to develop a course dealing with states of consciousness-- not usually offered in the psychology curriculum at most colleges. He planned to include material on sleep and dreaming, hypnosis, and drug-induced states both psychological and biological issues. Morris was familiar with recently published research on "lucid dreams," conducted at the Sleep Research Laboratory at Stanford University and presented those findings in his lectures. Lucid dreams are those in which the dreamer knows he is asleep, is able to influence the content of the dream, and can terminate the dreaming at will. Not everyone who attempts to elicit such dreams is successful. Many of those who are, enjoy eliciting dreams of flying, which they describe as a very pleasant experience. Morrie had

attempted to produce such dreams himself. The method

involves simply thinking about what you wish to dream

just prior to falling asleep. The closest Morrie had come

was when he, too, tried to dream he was flying. He was

only partially successful. Instead of producing images of

spreading his arms and gently soaring above the clouds,

he dreamed he was flying with Irv, his closest friend, in

Irv's Cesna. It was a reliving of an actual experience

some time earlier, one which was not particularly

pleasant for Morrie. Rather than being relaxed, Morrie

sat white knuckled in the rear seat during the entire flight.

However, it did convince him that lucid dreams were

possible, even if he wasn't very good at it.

Now that was teaching about the phenomenon

ancd encouraging his students to try the procedure,

Morrie thought he should try it himself one more. Again

the experiment produced unexpected results, but these were more dramatic.

Morrie retired at his usual time. Naomi was watching a late night movie. This time Morris concentrated on a vivid image of himself floating in the air, sans airplane.

As he drifted off to sleep he held that image as long as he could. It requires about an hour to descend through the various stages of sleep stages to REM sleep. During this phase there are certain physical changes that a scientist can measure, signifying that the sleeper is dreaming. The most distinguishing consists of rapid eye movements (hence REM) as if watching a tennis match. Of course, Morris was oblivious to the passage of time. Had he been attached to the appropriate instrumentation, an observer would be aware of him dreaming. Morrie's dream imagery was unlike any dream he had ever encountered, either during his own sleep or listening to the dream

recollections of his patients.

Morrie felt himself leaving his body and rising

toward the ceiling of the room. He could clearly see

himself still lying peacefully in his bed. He recognized

that he not only could see but could hear himself

breathing. His body was curiously still. Usually he was a

restless sleeper. He told himself that the lack of motion

was due to the muscular paralysis that occurs in the

voluntary muscle system during REM sleep. He also

found he could guide his movements. It seemed perfectly

natural to him that he was weightless.

He became aware that he was now having first hand

evidence that mind or soul can exist external to an

organic body and nervous system. He must make note of

that when he returned to a natural state.

16

Time Warp

Morrie kept the out-of-body experience to himself. He tried not to deal with the question of whether the entire episode was a dream or more than that. He was uneasy about falling asleep the next night and when he did finally drop off it was while willing himself not to dream.

A week went by uneventfully before Morrie finally let his curiosity prevail and he again focused on images of flying upon retiring. The transition occurred more rapidly on this occasion, although Morrie could not be aware of that. He guided his flight farther on this occasion, testing the limits of his newfound powers. He found he could travel through walls, but it was less disconcerting to go around objects. He also tried to interact with people but they appeared to be oblivious of him. He guided his flight to the Split Rail Farm. Jeremy was seated by the fire reading, a glass of bourbon by his side. Morrie called out to him. Jeremy seemed to stir but clearly could not see him and did not respond. Morrie moved on. From somewhere in his unconscious, and with out prior planning, Morrie imagined traveling back in time. Impulsively, with abandon, he willed it, without specifying or even giving thought to have far back in time he should trave

***

The old man appeared startled at first but then accepted his sudden appearance without signs of concern. His skullcap and prayer shawl indicated that he was Jewish and the finery of his clothing suggested he was a religious dignitary—likely a rabbi. Yet there was also something about him that suggested a Moslem or Arabian influence. Unlike the others Morris had encountered in his bodiless wanderings, this man was well aware of his presence. He spoke to Morrie without words, as if in prayer. Morrie could understand him clearly.

"Are you the spirit of a deceased person, my son?"

"No Rabbi. I am alive but my spirit is wandering as I lay sleeping. I am from a future time."

"I am known as Rambam. Do you know of me?"

"What century is this, Rabbi?"

This is the twelfth century by your reckoning."

Morrie searched his memory banks. His education in Judaism was spotty at best and it was many years since he had been exposed to Talmudic law. Yet the name Rambam had some meaning to him.

"Are you the esteemed Jewish sage, Maimonides?

Morrie was impressed with his knowledge and that he could access it so easily.

"I am Moses ben Maimon (son of Maimon), rabbi and physician to the Sultan of Egypt and his family. Yet there are many who dispute my writings and philosophy, even among my own people."

"In my time, Rabbi, you are regarded as the most influential Jewish thinker of the Middle Ages, and perhaps of all time."

***

Maimonides was born to a wealthy family in Cordoba, Spain under Moorish rule.

He was educated by his father in Jewish law but also read extensively the works of Muslem and Greek philosophers. He acquired a distaste for mysticism and an appreciation of scientific knowledge. When the Moors conquered Cordoba, Jews and Christians had the choice of conversion to Islam, death, or exile. Maimonides fled with his family, first to Morocco and then to Egypt. The family lost most of their fortune and Mainmonides, forced to earn money, began practicing medicine.

Maimonides's major contribution was the Mishneh Torah, a summary of Jewish law. The Mishneh Torah was written as a guide to Jews on how to behave in all situations. Maimonides was criticized by many traditional Jews , who feared that people would rely solely on his digest and no longer study the Talmud. To this day, however, Maimonides is one of the most widely studied Jewish scholars. His teachings also influenced the non-Jewish world. His philosophy is regarded as a convergence of Greco-Roman, Arab, Jewish, and Western culture.

***

"Why did you seek me out?

"I didn't. It just happened."

"But you were seeking something."

"I have had some strange things happen to me...of a spiritual nature."

"You were drawn here for a reason. Du bist Yiddish? (You are Jewish?")

Yes, Rabbi, but I am not observant."

"That is unfortunate. What is your Hebrew name?"

"Moshe."

"Then you are part of the lineage."

"So I have strayed."

"There are many paths to the truth."

"You believe in the existence of one God?"

"I have doubted many times but basically I believe in an omnipotent, all powerful God."

"You are a righteous man? You follow the commandments?"

"I have tried to help people who are troubled."

"Then you do God's work."

"Would you answer some questions?"

"You have traveled a long way. I will try."

"If God is good, why is there evil?"

"Evil is the lack of the presence of God in those who choose to reject Him."

"There are those who seek life meaning in the position of the stars."

"I have studied astrology s a young man and reject what cannot be established by rational proof. Man's destiny is not determined by the stars."

"Is there a soul without a body?"

"Are you not here, now?"

"I may be dreaming I am here."

"There is a soul that transcends earthly matter. "

"Then what is soul?"

"It is the essence of our efforts to attain absolute, pure knowledge of God".

"Can there be resurrection?"

"The afterlife does not consist of bodies being raised from the grave. Such belief is folly. The righteous soul can be immortal. If resurrection does occur, it is purely immaterial."

"Rabbi, when will the Messiah arrive?"

"When you are ready for it."

"When will that be, Rabbi. We have waited long.and suffered much"

"When there is universal righteousness."

"May I have your blessing, Rabbi?"

"A blessing on your head, Moshe."

17

Of Wandering Souls

Morrie decided to research the history and evidence for disembodied spirits. Throughout history man has reported unusual experiences that defy belief, cannot be easily explained, and seem to confirm the existence of a spirit that can leave the body, both before and after death. Every culture has its shamans who claim to have the power to invoke such phenomena. Medicine men from Native American tribes claimed the ability to leave their bodies in a state of trance and to communicate with supernatural beings or to escort the recently deceased to the after world. Medieval witches were believed to have the power of flight, sometimes on broomsticks. The witches were believed to communicate with the devil, sometimes in the form, of a goat. Much of the evidence for these happenings came from persons being tortured. The use of hallucinogenic drugs by both the Indian shamans and the witches may have provided the perception of leaving the body and flying. Belief in rebirth and reincarnation is found in many cultures. Celtic peoples believed that the soul traveled from body to body for all eternity. Egyptian pharaohs prepared for death their entire life. Buddhists believe in an endless cycle of rebirth until the individual reaches a state of nirvana, a condition of ultimate enlightenment and freedom from desire. Modern day psychics find proof for the spirit leaving the body in what has been labeled out-of-body experiences (OBE) or astral travel, and near death experiences (NDE).

Individuals reporting out-of-body excursions may bring back information to which they had no prior access.. Some believers assert that having the soul leave the body is risky since evil spirits may take possession of an unoccupied body. Medically afflicted patients may use OBE to escape unbearable pain. Victims of torture have reported the same mechanism. A more parsimonious explanation of OBE is that they are hallucinations or lucid dreams.

There are also reports of persons pronounced clinically dead—usually brain dead—who are suddenly and unexpectedly revived. The reports of NDE are remarkably similar. Such visions of the afterlife have occurred throughout history. In these cases individuals report experiencing themselves leaving their body and being able to look down upon themselves. They are able to move around effortlessly. They feel pain free and often a sense of sublime peace. They see themselves entering a dark tunnel with a light at the end. Often there is someone there to greet them. They may be deceased relatives or Jesus. Others see themselves in Heaven with beautiful flowers, rivers and streams. Sometimes they meet God. They are then commanded to go back, which they do, sometimes reluctantly. Many individuals who are revived after seemingly clinical death report a drastic change in their lives and the absence of a fear of death. They become more spiritual, although not necessarily more religious, and less materialistic.

Some neuroscientists explain NDEs as the result of a dying brain. The visual cortex, deprived of stimulation, provides flashes of light and darkness that may be perceived as a tunnel and lightness. They theorize that all the pleasurable sensations during an NDE are a kind of wish fulfillment. The last flicker of consciousness produces a desirable scenario—something it would like to experience. This phenomenon may represent an inborn mechanism to help us cope with the trauma of death. Advanced resuscitation technology probably makes NDEs more frequent. The reality of what really happens with NDE remains primarily a matter of faith, not objective evidence.

Morrie remained between dilemma's horns.

18

A Worry

Naomi cringed as the oncologist plunged the needle into her breast. She had felt the lump a few days ago and seen her gynecologist immediately. A mammogram confirmed the presence of the foreign body. She had to wait a week for the appointment with the oncologist. She hadn't told Morrie yet. She thought it would be best to wait for the lab results. It was enough that she was terrified. Better to wait until she knew. Besides, he had been so distant lately...preoccupied with something he hadn't shared with her. They had been married three years--a second go 'round for both of them. She was a widow. He had been divorced. Each had grown children. She worried that the magic had faded. Neither had rushed into the relationship. He was busy with his private practice; she was also immersed with her job at the school district. They enjoyed traveling together and they shared their work experiences   When they finally married and moved to their present house it had seemed so right.   Now she no longer was certain. He seemed depressed and she didn't know how to deal with it.   Whatever the outcome, she would have to tell him about the lump.

When she arrived home Morrie was waiting for her.. He knew something was wrong by the look on her face.

"What's the matter? You look like you were hit by a train."

"I have a lump. I've known about it for a week. I didn't want to worry you. I had a biopsy today. I'll hear tomorrow."

Morrie was consumed with worry and guilt. He knew he had been ignoring her for no good reason. And now this.

"I'm so sorry. I'm here for you whatever the results. We'll deal with this together.

She collapsed sobbing in his arms.

***

Not all worry is justified and not all lumps are cancer. Naomi dodged the bullet on this occasion. Her lump was a cyst. It would have to be watched by more frequent mammograms and self-examination but for now no treatment was necessary.

From that point Morris started to change. He vowed to communicate better with his wife, to share his extraordinary experiences as well as the more mundane parts of his existence. They drew closer and life settled back to a more normal routine. They promised to spend more time traveling and enjoying life and making the most of retirement. Naomi cut back her work hours to part time, saving the latter part of the week for extended weekends.

Insofar as his nighttime excursions, Morris assumed a more philosophical, yet pragmatic posture. He could not explain what had happened to him. Unlike with dream content, he retained a vivid recollection of all that had transpired. He did not rule out further sleep wanderings but he would not let it take over his life. He would place further obsessing on hold for a while as he attempted to integrate and consolidate what was going on psychologically. Yet he did not rule out future excursions. The "conversation" with Maimenides exerted a profound influence on him. He spent time at the local library reading as much as he could about the sage who continued to influence those who succeeded him. He might even join a study group on Judaism at Temple Israel. As for dealing with the issue of disembodied mind or soul, he was able to compartmentalize. His professional life, his training, his faith in empirical science remained intact. That it appeared inconsistent with his newfound spiritual interests was not a unique contradiction. Thinkers have tried to reconcile science and religion for centuries. Even Mainmenides embraced scientific understanding and rational thought and scoffed at the more literal interpretations of biblical stories—the "finger of God," for example. He was critical of astrology, decrying assertions of others that we are influenced by the stars. So, for the moment, Morrie, like countless others before him, would separate the two realms of science and religion, mind and body, physics and metaphysics.

19

Savannah

True to his resolve to travel more, Morrie and Naomi set out for Savannah. It was a long drive but they were in no hurry. The booked a suite at the Hilton in the old city. Neither had ever been to Savannah. Morrie had preconceptions about the old south but found his apprehensions completely unfounded. They both were charmed by the beauty and friendliness of the city. They walked from square to square, took the trolley tour, de-boarding at interesting areas and re-boarding the next car. They did the river walk by day and the Savannah River Gospel river boat tour in the evening. They drove to the old cemetery and were surprised at the large Jewish population. They toured the First Baptist church which had been a station on the underground railroad They spent a day on the beach at Tybe Island. Finally they booked the ghost walk which occurs after dark by lantern light.   The guide related numerous ghost stories of the area and they walked to allegedly haunted houses. Given his earlier experiences and new found, new age openness, Morris half expected to see a few apparitions. While he reacted to the stories wit skepticism, Morrie was secretly disappointed. Not even a cold shiver. Though Savannah had a rich history and a reputation for harboring ghosts, there would be no disembodied spirits for him in this city—not even in the cemetery.

20

Benidictus

Morrie felt confident enough to attempt another OBE. His mind was open to whatever it brought. He would refrain from drawing any conclusions about he was truly embarking on a spiritual voyage or merely enjoying some neurological aberration producing brain misfiring. He resolved to enjoy the experience whatever its origins and to learn from it if possible. Again, he had no particular destination but would attempt to go back in time.

***

The man seated before him was longhaired and dressed in garments reminiscent of paintings Morris remembered of the early Dutch settlers of New Amsterdam. He was seated at a work table grinding lenses, apparently for spectacles.

Morrie spoke first, startling the artisan, who was absorbed in his thoughts.

"Excuse me, sir. A moment of your time."

"You speak Yiddish?"

"I understand a little but I don't speak it well. Can you speak English?

"I speak several languages. You are an Anglisher?

"No I am from America. My name is Morris Schwartz. Can you tell me the year?"

"You mock me. Even in the New World they revile me."

"I mean you get no disrespect. I have traveled a long distance and need to orient myself."

"You are in The Hague, the Netherlands. It is 1676. I am known here as Benedictus de Spinoza. I was born Baruch."

"Meaning blessed."

"Yes. My fellow Jews do not consider me blessed here. I was expelled from the Dutrch Jewish community because of my beliefs and writing."

"I am from another time but I know of you Baruch Spinoza. You are considered one of the great philosophers of the 17th century, perhaps the greatest Jewish philosopher ever. Your ideas laid the groundwork for the rational philosophy of the next century."

"I am sick now, Morris Schwartz. I cough constantly. The dust from these infernal lenses has damaged my lungs. I fear I have little time left."

"You are familiar with Maimonides?"

"He was a significant influence on my thinking—a rebel, like myself."

"Why are your own people so against you?"

"I reject their ritual and am critical of parts of the Talmud. Mine is not the personal God of Abraham, Isaac and Joseph. God is nature and all is God. I do not accept the Bible as a source of revelation. I do not accept how Judaism is practiced or any other religion for that matter."

"In my time we label your belief Pantheism. God is in all things."

"That makes it seem that God is in all things when really it is the other way around. There is only one substance and that is God."

"Why is there evil in the world if everything is God?"

"God is perfect. Everything must be as it is. Things cannot happen otherwise.
God causes everything to happen. Right and wrong, good and evil are only our perceptions. It is only our selfishness that creates these distinctions"

"Everything is determined."

"Yes, there is no free will, but there is also no purpose. God doesn't do things to bring about some end."

"Why not?"

"Because that would imply that things are not perfect to begin with, that things need to be better, or that something should exist that doesn't."

"Tell me Baruch. Is it possible that spirit, mind, consciousness exist external to the body?"

"Foolish ideas proposed by Descartes. There is no dualism. Mind and body are one and the same, a single entity. The physical and mental worlds are one and the same."

"Then I am speaking to you as both a body and a mind."

"Of course."

"Does God exist as a personality?"

"There is no personality. God is the natural world."

"'And what of man, of individual thought. Descartes reasoned, 'I think, therefore I am.'"

God is eternal and infinite. Our existence is inconsequential—a ripple on the surface of God."

At this Spinoza returned to his work and Morrie was back in his body, perhaps a little wiser. ..or just more confused.

21

Back to the Bronx

Once Morrie was able to accept his OBEs without constantly challenging their validity he was able to enjoy them. He grew accustomed to his newfound freedom from his body and the physical laws attached to it and was more motivated to go back in time than to explore the here and now. He actually tried to project himself into the future but had no success. "I guess Christmas past is more accessible," he mused. Too bad, I'd love to peak at next month's stock page." However, his newfound nonchalance was more fragile than he thought when he realized where his astral wanderings had taken him on the next attempt.

**

Morrie was hovering near the ceiling in his old apartment in the Bronx. He was in the living room. He immediately recognized the plush red living room carpet that showed the sweeper tracks and the upright RCA radio in the corner. There was Sarah, his mother, as she looked when Morrie was about seven. She looked prettier than he remembered at that age. No signs of the grey hair he knew from later years. He felt indescribable joy in seeing her once more. If only Sydney, his father, was there as well, but he must have been at work. He tried to reach out, to touch her but she was oblivious of his presence. He turned his attention to the boy she was scolding. The likeness was that of his childhood photographs. He was clearly looking at his childish personae. His hair was parted on the side and falling into eyes. He was holding a toy silver airplane in his hand. He remembered that toy vividly. It had propellers on the wings that turned and landing gears that folded up. The plane was the source of the scolding. Sarah was chastising him for stealing the plane from his next door neighbor, Beanie. She was dragging him back to

Beanie's apartment to return the plane and apologize for filching it. He saw himself fumbling to find the right words and felt his own humiliation at the time as if it were happening now. It was a strange experience because he also was able to evaluate what was unfolding. There was more to the story. The plane had been his originally. He kept it in his toy chest in his room. Beanie had been playing at his house with the plane and admired it. Sara pointed out that Morris had many planes and encouraged him to let Beanie have the toy. Morrie had been angry and hurt but complied. The next day at Beanie's house his resentment at being made to relinquish his prize possession overwhelmed him. He sneaked the plane into the pocket of his knickers and brought it him. Sarah saw it, realized what Morrie had done, and began reprimanding him. Morrie completely identified with his younger self. He wanted to intervene. He wanted young Morrie to explain to his mother how much he coveted that plane. None of his other planes were as sleek, as realistic. He had dreamed about that plane, flying over his house and then landing at his feet. It's size was exactly as it looked in the air. Morrie wanted to put words in his childhood mouth, already showing signs of the oversized protruding teeth that would later require orthodontia. He tried to intervene and change things but found he could only observe. This was not Maimonides or Spinoza, whom he could talk with readily. Strange happenings, indeed.

Back in a wakened state, Morrie examined the implications of this latest OBE. Assuming he was not hallucinating, and not having lucid dreams, what did his vision reveal? Clearly there must be some energy, some force field that transcends time. In some sense it is there. Can it be that every experience we have is not time limited but persists for all eternity in what philosophers once called the "ether." This would certainly imply a different concept of reality. If he can conjure up past experiences that appear as lifelike as when they actually occurred then how do identify what is real. He was already doubting his senses, his perceptions. How can he know whether his vision is reality and his waking existence merely an illusion. If his consciousness is something beyond neural activity but rather "out there" is it also accessible to others? Is it like an EEG or a PET scan that others can tap as accurately as its electrical or chemical properties? If an immaterial "mind" external to the body, then Descartes and Plato were right in assuming a dualism and Spinoza was wrong. It would explain the sometimes uncanny sensitivities of some people to discern one's became excited as if on the verge of discovering a fundamental principle of the universe. And what of his psychology that he spent a career pursuing—his science that had evolved from philosophy and progressed from armchair introspection to empirical behavioral research? Are the real answers to be provided by the philosophers after all? Or is it the psychics who will lead us to the truth? Morrie's new-found comfort thought, so show empathy. It would explain what happened to him in Sedona. Morrie with his astral wanderings was shaken again.

22

It's All Relative

Morrie found himself on a college campus. Walking along a long path in front of him was a familiar character. The old man wore a long winter overcoat and fur cap against the winter chill. His long, uncombed hair made identification certain.

"Good evening Professor Einstein. May I walk with you?"

"Nu, life is like riding a bicycle. To keep your balance you've got to keep moving. I wrote that once to my son Eduard. You are a teacher here?

"No Professor. It's hard to understand but I am from another time."

"That is not an impossibility. Time is not absolute. Some of my physicist friends believe an object can even be in two places at once."

"I have read about quantum mechanics professor. I believe you laid the groundwork for the concept but you are now a disbeliever"

"Then you may also know I have been working for many years on a unified theory that would restore certainty and determinism to physics."

"You have criticized probability concepts."

"God doesn't play dice with the universe."

"Professor. I am searching for answers about mind or soul, about God."

"You are a religious man?"

"I am a cultural Jew. I do not actively practice my religion but I identify with Judaism and with the state of Israel."

"So you are a bit of a rebel, like me. I, too, did not adhere to the rituals. Yet I identify strongly with the Jewish people and with Zionism. You know I was offered the Presidency of Israel but I turned it down. The

Jew who abandons his faith is like the snail who abandons his shell. He is still a snail."

"So how does God fit into your theoretical system?"

"God manifests himself in the beauty and harmony of nature's laws. I believe in a spirit that is larger than ourselves. The pursuit of science produces a special awe that is my religious feeling."

"Your ideas are reminiscent of a philosopher who was excommunicated from the

Jewish community for expressing such heresy."

"Baruch Spinoza was a great influence on me."

"What other philosophers did you draw upon?"

"Hume also believed time was relative. He emphasized the importance of perceptions and observations in forming concepts."

"To be is to be perceived."

"I don't go that far. I believe in absolute and invariant laws of nature."

"You learned to appreciate empirical research but you didn't conduct experiments yourself."

"I tend to see concepts visually. I reason things out in thought experiments.
Immanual Kant awakened me to the importance of reasoning in discerning truths."

"What today we refer to as deductive v. inductive reasoning."

"Yes. But remember it was I that proposed the experiment that confirmed general relativity. The experiment proved that light rays can be bent by gravity."

"Your name is associated with many important papers and discoveries. It is synonymous with the concept of relativity. Your equation showing the relationship between matter and energy provided the basis for atomic energy. I believe you wrote to President

Franklyn Roosevelt to develop the atomic bomb. What would you label as your most important contribution?."

"For nearly three hundred years the prevailing concepts in physics were based on the mechanical universe of Sir Isaac Newton. It was based on absolute certainties and laws. I found that Newtonian physics did not explain many phenomena. In my concept of the universe space and time are dependent upon frames of reference. I continue to work on a broad based unified field theory that will encompass everything from the motions of the smallest particles to the galaxies."

" Field theory. That term was used by Gestalt psychologists to include the forces present in the environment to interact with personality variables in predicting behavior."

"Yes, I met once with Max Wertheimer from Swarthmore College and we exchanged ideas."

"What is your impression of psychology as a science?"

"It is important to explore our subjective world but it is at present hopelessly difficult, even for Einstein."

"How did you arrive at the notion of physical field theory?"

"I was a young boy when I became fascinated by the action of forces upon a compass needle, swinging it toward the north. The existence of these invisible forces left a deep and lasting impression me. When I was 16   I pondered about the speed of light. If you could ride along a light beam at the speed of light, wouldn't the light waves seem stationary to you? "

"So you were already thinking of things as relative, not absolute."

"I refined that thought experiment later. I was able to reason that two lightning bolts striking a train, one at each end, would seem to arrive simultaneously to a viewer on the embankment at the middle of the train. However, a passenger at the midpoint of the train would see the bolt in front slightly ahead of the bolt in the rear, because he was moving toward it. Thus two events that appear to be simultaneous to one stationary observer will not appear simultaneous to another observer who is moving rapidly. There is no way to declare which observer is really correct. In other words there is no way to determine if events are truly simultaneous. That was my thought experiment to describe special relativity."

"The thought experiment makes a difficult concept understandable, Professor."

"Aha. Now you have insight."

"I have been trained to think rationally but I am torn between my scientific training and my spiritual needs."

"Remember, my friend, science without religion is lame; religion without science is blind."

"I have taken enough of your time, Dr. Einstein. Just one last question. Are you really here at Princeton talking with me or is this just an aberration of my nervous system?"

"Ah, we are back to David Hume. Is anything real or just our perception of reality. Perhaps this quest of yours is why you are here talking to me. Go back, my friend, and read Hume and Kant on this issue.

23

Entering a Transit

"The act of passing over, across, or through; the conveyance of persons or goods from one place to another; a transition or change, especially from one life to another at death; in astronomy the passage of a celestial body across the observer's meridian; the passage of a smaller celestial body across the disc of a larger celestial body; a surveying instrument that measures horizontal and vertical angles."

Although Morrie knew the definition of the word "transit," he wanted to be sure of the precise meaning. He also used the dictionary to define "astrology."

"The study of positions and aspects of heavenly bodies with a view to predicting their influence on the course of human affairs."

Beneath "astrology" the dictionary defined "astrometry," a word with which Morrie was unfamiliar,

"The scientific measurement of the positions and motions of celestial bodies."

Astrology is a pseudoscience, Morris told himself. There isn't a shred of evidence to support the belief that the positions of the planets or stars at the time of one's birth or at any time thereafter has the slightest influence upon personality or behavior. His years of training and in his own early attempts at research indelibly impressed upon the psychologist how weak the statistical associations of most variables were with human behavior. Even when correlations were statistically significant (meaning that the differences obtained when those variables were present as opposed to when they were not) the relationships accounted for only a small fraction of the total variability in behavior. In addition, correlations do not establish cause and effect. There are usually many possible explanations of why two variables will co-vary, most completely unrelated to the particular hypothesis or theory of the experimenter. Psychological concepts, even those most universally accepted, were based on probabilities, not certainty. The supposition that planetary orbits and crossings control our fate is absurd.

Morrie knew all this before consulting the dictionary. The acceptance of astrology as a science by millions of people made as much sense as accepting that Elvis was still alive or that Geller could bend spoons without touching them. Yet, in a whimsical and curious mood when surfing the Internet, he had typed in the word "astrology." When one link offered a free reading, requiring only a birth-date, Morrie took the bait and responded. Despite his skepticism, the return e-mail came as a surprise.

Since ancient times astrologers have held that the movements of heavenly bodies determine our destinies. Some even believe that astrological readings can reveal past lives and reincarnations. Rudolph Steiner, a nineteenth century German philosopher believed that

after death the soul journeyed around the planets prior to

its reincarnation on earth. Some astrologers have

examined birth and death charts of well known persons

and linked them to similar charts of well known deceased

persons.

Morrie's astrological reading, three pages in

length, was almost convincing. The astrologer, Catlyn,

acknowledged his response and made it clear that the

Astral Bodies

were highly explicit about his future. She indicated that

she felt a strong connection to Morrie. This bond made it

easy for her to read his feelings and plot his destiny. She

indicated that Morrie was in a period of change in his

life—a change that had already begun. She believed him

to be a highly sensitive person, respected for his wisdom,

who appreciates and needs this respect. She indicated

that he likes to be with people his own age or younger.

She saw him as "streetwise" and disdainful of those with only book learning. She implied that he was entering a rare and highly propitious transit of 72 days. This period was a rare event and likely not to recur over a very long period of time. The opportunities provided during this transit included very positive financial changes. These would occur as a result of some game of chance or lottery. However, he must act in a very certain way at a specified time. For a fee she would send a very comprehensive and detailed analysis that would specify his exact course of action. . Should he avail himself of present opportunities, it would change the remainder of his life and allow him to complete a project he had been working on for several months.

Morrie was surprised by the accurate reading of life change, which could reflect his adjustment to retirement and relocation. Nevertheless, his cynicism prevailed. After several days he returned to the reading , which he had printed, analyzed it further, then severed his relationship with the astrologer

The predictions, he concluded, were of three types: those that were accurate and specific; those that were so broad they could apply to anyone; those that were blatantly wrong. It was true that he was in a period of transition in his life. She could discern that from his age. Yes, he was regarded as wise and craved respect. If age brings wisdom, then she didn't need a crystal ball for that prediction and most people crave respect. That he preferred to be with people his own age or younger was a safe bet since most people were younger than Morrie. To call him streetwise and critical of book-learning was certainly inaccurate. Furthermore, the report was extremely redundant. One paragraph was replicated verbatim. It was clear to Morris that the report was a cut and paste job on the computer. Years of supervising beginning psychologists and interns made him keenly

aware of boiler plate.

Nevertheless he bought a lottery ticket from a

machine at the supermarket. He won two dollars.

24

Unconscious

The room looked strangely familiar. The
Victorian sofa covered by a heavy blanket, the lamps on
tables with crocheted cloths. And then it came to him.
He recognized the room from photographs he had seen
many times. This was the consulting room where
psychoanalysis originated. It was perhaps around 1920
and he was visiting the illustrious Dr. Sigmund Freud in
Vienna. It all made sense. His earlier astral wanderings
shared some common elements. Maimonides, Spinoza,
and Einstein were all Jewish, were rebels, and were
innovators. They had pit themselves against the
establishment. All had exerted a lasting influence upon
the history of religious and scientific thought. Why not,
then, confront another of their ilk and one more
connected to his own profession. Although Morrie was
not aware of any purposeful choice on this excursion,

somehow he had made the selection and it was supremely logical.

When the old man entered the room there was no question as to his identity.

"Good evening Dr. Freud."

"You are my next patient? I was not expecting you."

"I am a visitor from far off, Doctor. Would you grant me a few moments of your time?"

"I have been in my study, writing. Would you like a cup of tea?"

"No, Doctor. Just a few questions. Your writings have exerted an influence far beyond what you may have imagined."

"I have my critics, even those I trained to carry on the work."

"Ideas change, Dr. Freud. The science moves on. Your insights have influenced a major revolution in the way we think of personality. Your predecessors searched for traits and types of personality—all static and immutable. You described personality as a dynamically interacting forces."

"You came to question me. Yet, you seem knowledgeable. Let me ask you one question. What do you consider my major contributions?"

Your emphasis upon the Unconscious and its influence upon personality and behavior, your awareness of conflict between opposing parts of the personality, your description of the major defenses of the ego, a topic your daughter Anna has also explored, your description of the developmental stages of personality and their influence upon adult personality, your analysis of the meaning of dreams."

"You are indeed well read and conversant with my thinking. You mention areas I am still developing. You are an analyst?"

"I have been analyzed but my training has led me in different directions. Your work has spawned many offshoots, both here in Europe and across the sea."

"Yah, I lectured to the Americans at Clark University in 1909 at the invitation of Dr. Hall. You have read my Introductory Lectures?"

"I have. A later version. A tremendous influence on American psychology."

"I traveled with Jung. We were still friends at that time. But you Americans go off in superficial directions. This behaviorism. It is non-consequential. You miss the importance of intrapsychic events."

"They believed that if you can't see it or measure it then it is not science."

"Then thoughts and feelings and unconscious motivation are to be ignored?"

"Not by many of my contemporaries."

"And your questions to me?"

"You were first a physician and neurologist. Do you still hold to the importance of the physical workings of the body in determining psychic phenomena?"

"First there is the nervous system. All else follows."

"And after death?"

"Alles ist kaput. There is no more."

"And your religion? Did you forsake it completely?"

"Religion is for the comfort of the ignorant and insecure. It evolves as other institutions do because it serves a purpose. It has given us our moral codes. But in the end man's aggressive heritage prevails to produce chaos. It will be the role of psychology to provide us ways of controlling our instincts but there will always be conflict. turmoil, and war It is our animal nature."

"Your parents were Jewish."

"Yah. They named me Schlomo. I changed it later to Sigmund."

And what of the larger questions…the universe..our origins. Do you believe the stars have an influence?"

"We cannot know. Our more immediate need is to understand our own psyche—to look inward for meaning. The universe will take care of itself."

"Is there no higher order of organization and influence, beyond our science, beyond our capacity to comprehend?"

"If it comforts you to believe so, I will not disillusion you."

At this the physician, turned therapist and philosopher, left the room."

25

Kabbalah

Morrie was settling into a routine. He had

compartmentalized his strange and unusual experiences.

After revealing them to Naomi, who regarded his time

travels as vivid dreams, Morrie was able to resume his

life. The year 2000 also settled back to normal after the

millennium hysteria over anticipated computer

catastrophes had proven to be overblown. There were

terrorist attacks all over the globe but from Morrie's

perspective the publication of the first draft of the human

genome in June was the year's most significant

accomplishment, which would preview future

breakthroughs. The mapping of human DNA would

provide answers not only to the treatment of hereditary

cancer, diabetes, and heart disease but to mental

conditions as well. Morrie had treated a criminal

psychopath whose evil roots lay not so much in his early environment but in his genes.

Morrie began attending his local synagogue on Saturday mornings and sometimes on Friday evenings as well. He had grown fond of Rabbi Hershman and his wife Rachel and they began seeing each other socially. One evening at a dinner at Morrie's the Rabbi surprised Morris by asking him to attend a study group dealing with Kabballah.

"Rabbi, I am shocked. Kabbalah is an unauthorized offshoot of Judaism, steeped in mysticism."

"I am not preaching it, Morrie, but I have long held an interest in early writings.
Rabbi Maimonides was a believer in Kabbalah and many others have followed. I have only an academic interest. Why don't you join us? I would appreciate your psychological insights."

"At the mention of Maimonides, Morrie was momentarily caught off guard.

He agreed to participate.

Kabbalah is an expression of Jewish mysticism. It includes a large body of speculation about the nature of God, creation, the soul, and the role of human beings. It also consists of meditation, mystical, esoteric and magical practices which are known only to a select few. Adherents believe that mastery of the Kabbalah brings man spiritually closer to God and insight into Creation. The word Kabbalah derives from the root "to receive," "to accept." It is also used synonymously with "tradition."

The first five books of the Old Testament, the Torah or law, are considered to be divine. According to Jewish tradition, Moses received the written law from God but also received the oral law, which was not written down from generation to generation. The Kabbalah is considered the oral law or oral tradition. The study of

Kabbalah leads to an understanding of hidden meanings

and the divine power they contain, including the secrets

of the creation. It is further believed that embedded in

the Kabbalah is the biblical power of prophecy

Kabbalistic knowledge has been transmitted orally by the

Jewish patriarchs, prophets, and sages. Many Kabbalists

believe that Kabbalah dates back to the Garden of Eden

and was preserved only by a privileged few. Others trace

its origins to Mount Sinai, about the 13th century BCE.

However, throughout history Kabbalah has been

interpreted, modified. Later generations of Kabbalists

speculated about many aspects of the Book of Genesis,

including the nature of God, Adam and Eve, The Tree of

Knowledge, Good and Evil, and the Tree of Life. The

bible provides ample material of mythical and mystical

material. Jacob's ladder, the burning bush, the parting of

the Red Sea, and the acceptance of the Torah on Mount

Sinai are such examples. The Hassidic movement in Judaism had roots in Kabbalah but Kabbalah is not limited to Hassidism. Some false prophets have used Kabbalah for monetary gain. Many people who study Kabbalah are not Jewish. Kabbalistic knowledge was kept secrete for fear that it would fall into the hands of enemies.

***

The group convened in the Rabbi's study. In addition to Morrie, it consisted of four elderly men who were long time members of the congregation. All were fluent in reading and translating Hebew. Rabbi Hershman was ready to convene the session, which was to explore a section of the *Sefer Zohar*, written at the end of the 13th century. The Zohar was the first truly popular work of Kabbalah, and the most influential. Although a medieval document, it reflects the rationalist influence of Maimonides to explain earlier esoteric subjects philosophically. The Rabi had selected several authoritative interpretations of the particular section to be studied—the ten *Sephiroth,* literally the ten "eminations," reveal ten levels of creation—ten different ways of revealing God. Morrie was beginning to regret that he agreed to participate. These old men were clearly Jewish scholars. His own background was limited to the ability to read Hebrew sufficiently to participate in services, usually without understanding. He began to contemplate how he could withdraw gracefully from the group. At the last moment a new arrival changed his mod from regret to a pleasant surprise. Jeremy Craig apologized to the group for being late. Unlike the others who were dressed as if for holiday services, Jeremy wore his usual jeans and flannel shirt.

Morrie could barely restrain his surprise at seeing his newfound friend.

"Jeremy, you never told me you were Jewish."

"Thought I might find you here. I'm not a member of the Tribe, Morrie.

I'm interested in the topic and when I saw the announcement in the local paper, I thought I'd give it a whirl. I hope it's OK with you Rabbi. I don't speak Hebrew."

"You're certainly welcome here. I'd appreciate your input"

"A "goyishe" (gentile) point of view." einterjected.

The group enjoyed the humor and it served as an icebreaker.

The Rabbi used the interlude as a segue to introductions. He asked each member why they were interested in Kabbalah. The others saw the group as a logical step in their exploration of the Torah and almost a duty to learn as much as possible about their religion. Morrie explained that he had a intellectual interest in the existence of soul and its relationship to a material body.

He chose not to mention anything about his out-of-body

experiences. Jeremy, who had drawn the interest of the

others, indicated that he had a more mystical interest. He

explained that he believed that he was a channel for

persons who were deceased He had read of the secrets

that that might may be revealed in the Torah and hoped it

might shed some light on his own experiences. The

others looked incredulous but tolerant of their Gentile

visitor.

The first night's discussion centered on the nature

of God and its relationship to the human soul. Rabbi

Hershman outlined some basic principles of Kabbalah.

God is defined as infinite and largely hidden from human

understanding. He can be revealed to man in a limited

way through his creations. The physical universe is made

of Divine Light, which can be construed in modern

physics as energy. "The human soul," the Rabbi

explained (and here Morrie listened intently) "is part of the Creator (Divine Light). Therefore, there is no difference between God and the soul. He is the whole and the soul a part. God is neither matter nor spirit but the creator of both. Human consciousness is an aspect of Divine Consciousness, not a function of the brain. Certain aspects of God are accessible to human consciousness; other aspects are unknowable. The Zohar stipulates that the soul has three elements. One part is found in all humans and is given to us at birth. It is the source of our physical and psychological nature. It allows some awareness of the existence and presence of God. The other two parts can be developed over time and are related to our actions and beliefs. They exist fully in people who are awakened spiritually.

This introduction led to a heated discussion about the substance of God, the pre-existence of matter, and the origins of God. The topic became more abstract and metaphysical and Morrie lost interest.

After the meeting Morris and Jeremy stopped for a cup of coffee. Morrie expressed his reservations about the experience.

"I have trouble with philosophical speculation. There is no answer to the questions they raise. Even Kabbalists disagree among themselves."

"Is that what you want here, easy answers?"

"Easy, hard. Something I can sink my teeth into. It's all so flimsy."

"Give it a chance. You've just started."

""They will go on arguing forever."

"Perhaps you should change your perspective. Instead of school, consider this experience a process. It makes you think, helps you define yourself. Your answers have to come from within. If they label that Divine Consciousness" so be it."

"How did you get so wise?"

"Riding my tractor. How come you didn't reveal your psychic nature?"

"I've had some weird experiences that seem to be out-of-body. There are other explanations."

"Do you communicate with anyone during these travels?"

"I go back in time. I talk with historical figures. They talk back."

"Morrie, perhaps it is not you that is traveling but those you converse with."

"What do you mean?"

"I think you, like me, are a channel. They reach out from another dimension and talk through you."

"Like my automatic writing? Jeremy, that is outlandish."

"Yes, it is, but people have reported incidents of apparent channeling for thousands of years."

"Annecdotal evidence. Mediums act as intermediaries for spirits trying to communicate with someone." New Age fantasy, like reincarnation."

"It is difficult to document the claims of channelers, since the spirits that are channeling are usually obscure persons. Does it matter whether the entity communicating is really a departed person or merely the unconscious mind of the channeler? If they provide knowledge that promotes growth it can be valuable."

"You open up another can of worms with the unconscious."

"You're a psychologist. Don't you believe in the unconscious?

"We are not aware of many aspects of our thoughts or perceptions that may influence us. Freud's concept was based on a 19th century energy model. It's getting late Jeremy. Let's leave that discussion for another night."

"Are you coming back next week to Kabbalah?"

"Why not?"

26

Naomi

It had been a glorious few days as summer wound down. The temperature was cool in the evenings but rose to the mid-eighties during the day. It was too hot to walk except in the very early morning hours and after dusk. Morrie decided to sleep late after a restless night. Naomi arose early and decided to take an early mile-long stroll around McCloud's pond. The stars were still bright as the first streaks of sunlight poked tentatively over the eastern horizon. Naomi carried a flashlight to protect against the occasional car on the road but most people were still in bed. She wanted the time alone to collect her thoughts.

Naomi was becoming increasingly uneasy about Morrie and her marriage. Again he was becoming more isolated, more introspective. He was not sharing his thoughts with her and she felt reluctant to probe. Perhaps he needed his distance but she hated the feeling of being left out. On the occasions when she did confront him about it he became apologetic. He was preoccupied with his reading and his thoughts, he explained. It was nothing personal. He had begun Hebrew classes, in addition to his Kabbalah study group. True, she had her horses which were a great joy in her life. She was grateful to her husband for having provided the opportunity to fulfill a childhood dream. But she was concerned about Morrie's long hours pouring over parts of the Torah, sometimes mumbling to himself. It was not something they could share. Morrie was also with- drawing from his professional contacts and even his long time best friend Irv. It was a puzzle but she breathed in the refreshing precursor of an approaching fall and relaxed in the still cool night air. In the southeastern sky a radiant Venus in its eternal orbit graced the firmament.26

27

Afterlife

When does a mind cross the line? When does
fantasy become reality, hope become belief, self-
examination become self-deception. It was Yom Kipor,
the holiest of days when Jews reflect on the past year,
atone for their sins. The day is to be spent in *schul*,
fasting from sundown the evening before until sundown
the next day. It is a day of contemplation and prayer,
praying to be granted another year in the Book of Life.
Morrie, who had been attending services regularly was
not in synagogue. He was, however, contemplating about
life ands death and the hereafter. He had seen many
instances during his internship at the V.A. hospital of
hallucinations and delusions.
In the early 60s, when anti-psychotic medications were
first being introduced , he saw the full blown psychoses
not yet tempered by Thorazine. The old soldiers who

talked to their visions, listened to their commands,

persuaded themselves of their own grandeur.

What aberrant synapses predisposed these ordinary men

into their disturbed perceptions, deluded thoughts? What

environmental inputs triggered such aberrations? Morrie

recalled one incident when for a fleeting few instants he

also believed a dream image. It was the days of the

Cuban missile crisis. Kennedy had gone toe to toe with

the Russians who had supplied Castro with missiles.

Morrie was in the Army Reserves, having just completed

active duty. He was in his uniform, ready to attend the

weekly meeting at the Philadelphia Quartermaster Depot.

With about an hour to spare he lay down for a quick

catnap. He dreamed his unit had been activated and he

was about to leave for Cuba. He awakened and, realizing

he was in uniform, assumed the dream was real and he

was about to debark. Forebrain activity quickly resumed

control and he recognized what had happened. At the

time he reasoned that some similar mechanism must take

place with psychosis, when the environment confirms a

deep fear or wish. Now, in the first year of the new

millennium, was he again being deluded by his delving

into religion and mysticism?

Morrie realized he was becoming more atuned to

the growing infirmaties of aging. Fortunately his health

was still reasonably good but the stiffness in his back and

the slight hunch of his shoulders were constant reminders

of the growing arthritis and osteoporosis. His questions

about life's meaning and significance assumed more than

an academic interest. He pondered the question of an

afterlife, not only because of his bizarre psychic

experiences, but also an increasing awareness of his own

mortality. Both his parents had succumbed to cancer.

His chances of dying merely of old age were slight.

If there exists a soul independent of organic tissue, as the

prophets proclaimed, why not an afterlife when the body

is no longer viable? A recent research study Morris had read questioned people over fifty as to whether they believed in a life after death. Nearly two thirds of people surveyed indicated they did believe in an afterlife, women more so thgan men. Over 80% of believers also believe there is a Heaven, although fewer also believe in Hell. About a quarter of respondents believe in reincarnation. Those with lower incomes and less education were more likely to ascribe to an afterlife. Only a quarter of those studied agreed with the statement, "I believe that when I die, that's the end."

Half the group questioned also believed in ghosts.

The rise of mysticism occurred during the 1860s. Since then thousands, of mediums, psychics, and even scientists have tried to make contact with the departed. Many report success but usually because of personal experiences which cannot be replicated objectively, or because of chicanery. Anecdotal accounts of ghosts,

poltergeists, haunted houses, messages from beyond
abound and are popularized
in literature or the media. Native American cultures
accept the possibility of communication with the dead
through dreams, special ceremonies and drugs. Hindus
believe in reincarnation as part of the process of
achieving perfection over many lifetimes. Some
Kabbalists also believe in reincarnation but this concept
is rejected by those unwilling to identify with the more
magical aspects of mysticism.

Morrie had reached a point in his spiritual
development, unlikely in his younger years, where he was
open to such ideas and even experimentation. He clung
yet to his trust in scientifically validated laws but also to
Einstein's much quoted comment: "Science without
religion is lame; religion without science is blind." The
boundaries

between religious spirituality and mysticism were

tenuous.

28

Revelation

Rabbi Herschman was truly interested in spiritual enlightenment. He structured the study group toward discussions of meaningful understanding of the teachings of the Torah. His intent was not an abandonment of traditional Judaism but a deeper involvement in its moralistic implications. He wished to examine the development of Kabbalah over the centuries and to examine differences between the earliesr Talmudic era during the early centuries of the first millennium and later changes during the medieval and modern eras. Many orthodox Jews reject the idea that Kaballah underwent significant modification since the writing of the Zohar in the 13th century. But there are differences among the rabbis about such issues as the pre-existence of matter before there was a God. Did God create the matter of which the universe is made or did he use matter that was already there? The group pondered the existence of evil in the world. Is evil consistent with the notion of a compassionate and powerful God? Is there a dual nature of God—a good and evil side? Later texts talk of an "other side" of God which emanates forces that are the mirror image of the "side of holiness." They explored the ethical principles of Kabbalah and what makes righteous person. They discussed whether all parts of the Torah should be understood. Some of the rabbis cautioned that we have no business delving into secret things. There is increasing belief in mysticism and esotericism with the persecution of Jews during the Middle Ages, when Jews were being demonized as minions of Satan, during the Inquisition. Jews were also influenced by eastern and Christian theologies. Many looked for signs that the Messiah would soon come to comfort them. Many

Conservative and Reform groups reject the Kabbalah entirely as "worse than Christianity." Other groups like the Hassidim embrace the sacred texts.

Israel Rabinowitz, an older member of the group, had more than an academic interest in Kabbalah. For many years he had been enamored of the secret and even prophetic nature of the wisdom embedded in the scrolls. He had learned several of the methods of digit summing and had spent many hours pouring over selected portions of the Torah to decode hidden messages. One evening after the meeting he gave Morris a private lesson.

Kabbalah teaches that every Hebrew letter, word, number, and phrase of the Hebrew Bible contains a hidden meaning. The methods, called gematria, are also used by numerologists in other languages. Every letter is assigned a numerical value. The first letter, alpha, equals one. The second, beit, two, and so on. Summing these values for a word results in a 'key" for that word. Words

having the same key may be substituted for each other,

changing the meaning of the scripture. In one method the

numbers are reduced to one digit. The key 72 would be

9. It is assumed that these equivalences are not

coincidental. The world was created through God's

speech. Therefore every letter contains a creative force.

Equivalences reveal an internal connection between the

words and phrases.

***

Morrie was struggling with his Hebrew lessons.

Israel had advised him that gematria required a

knowledge of Hebrew so in addition to exploring

concepts he felt he back in Hebrew School preparing for

bar mitzvah.

Hebrew, like many other Semitic languages uses a

different alphabet. The Hebrew alphabet is called the

"alefbet" because of its first two letters, "alef" and "beit."

There are 24 letters, many of which sound like Greek and are in the same order as the Greek alphabet, because they are Greek derivatives. The early alefbet has no vowels And most things written in Hebrew do not use vowels. However, later sages recognized

the need for aids to pronunciation and added a system of dots and dashes above, below or inside the letter.

Israel and Morris were pouring over Exodus, the book of the bible describing the departure of the Israelites slaves from Egypt and the beginning of a forty year trek across the desert to the Promised Land. Moses leads his people over these years and is allowed by God to view his destination, but dies before reaching it. God has punished Moses in this way for showing a lack of faith when God instructed him how to obtain water from a rock. Moses strikes the rock twice, in doubt ,and is therefore not allowed to cross the Jordan.

Morrie learns from Israel that the name Moses

(Moshe), his namesake, drives in Hebrew from two

words, one meaning "water" and the other meaning "to

come out."

Moses had been set adrift in the Nile in a small boat made

of bulrushes by his mother to save his life. He was saved

by the Pharaoh's daughter and adopted by her.

However modern scholars consider the name as

symbolizing the deliverance from evil as God led his

people to the Promised Land. Water in the Bible is

sometimes considered a metaphor for evil. Some

scholars believe that the words derive from the Egyptian

language. "Mo" meant "water" and "Sa" meant "son,"

so Moses was the "son of water." The Egyptian words

may have later been translated to Hebrew.

Morrie (Moshe) Schwartz was shaken by this

knowledge. All his life he had harbored a fear of water.

Learning to swim in summer camp by being thrown out

of a boat in the middle of the lake may have been the origin of this fear. Numerous basement floods in his house after purchase perpetuated his concern about water and dreams if flooding signified anxiety from many sources. Was there some mysterious connection linking him to his biblical forbearer, other than the name itself? Morrie was beginning to place some credence in the power of numbers. The number "40" seemed to have significance in the Bible. It rained for 40 days and 40 nights when Noah built his arc. Moses and his tribe wandered 40 years in the desert. Morrie did the numerological calculation with his Hebrew name. The letter total of 340 was reduced to the number "7," following the rules. That number had it's own magical qualities

In 1956 psychologist George miller, an expert in communication theory, summarized research on the processing of informatioin by humans. It appears that our nervous systems impose severe limitations on the amount of information we can accurately process or remember at one time. In most experiments on judgment and memory the maximum number of dimensions or "chunks" we can remember is around seven. This applies to discriminations among musical tones, visual stimuli, or memory for digits. That is why telephone numbers (excluding area codes) are limited to seven digits. Miller points out numerous examples of the magic of sevens in our culture—the seven wonders of the world, the seven seas, the seven deadly sins, the seven ages of man, the seven levels of Hell, the seven primary colors, the seven notes of the musical scale, and the seven days of the week. "On the seventh day He rested." Miller asks, "Is there a deep and profound significance behind all those sevens or is it just a Pythagorean coincidence?"

29

Intervention

Naomi waited until Morrie was out of the house before she made the call. She found Irv's number in Morrie's Rolladex and carefully dialed the number. Irv Werlinski was Morrie's best friend, although he had not seen much of him since their move to the suburbs. He and Morrie had been graduate students together at Penn. They had been roommates in an apartment in West Philadelphia until Irv left to get married. They maintained their friendship over the years. Irv was also a clinical psychologist and they sporadically conferred on cases they were treating.

"Naomi, how are you? I haven't heard from Morrie in weeks. "

"That's why I'm calling you, Irv. It's Morrie. I think he's having a breakdown.   You're the only one I can confide in."

"That's hard to believe. He's always been the rock of Gibraltar. A little obsessive but he's always had a strong ego defense system."

"I know but things have changed since he retired. He's confided in me about some strange experience. I'm sure they were dreams and at first he was skeptical but he seems to have bought into it."

"Wait, slow down. You're going too fast. Start from the beginning."

"I don't know it all. He didn't share with me at first, I think it started when we visited Sedona and also the Grand Canyon. He had some mystical experiences. Then he got involved with . He was doing research."

"He knows better than that. There's no valid evidence for the claims."

"He resisted it but now he's reading Kabbalah, spending more and more time with numerology."

"There are a lot of phony rabbis selling bogus products."

"He knows that but he's become close with the rabbi out here who is a Kabbalah student…and he has a new friend who shares his interest. He's spending more and more time with this and withdrawing from everything else. I don't know where it will lead.

I just know he's having a crisis and a personality change. Can you come and talk with him?

"Invite me to dinner and don't tell him you've confided in me."

***

It was the first time Irv had been out to the Schwartz's new home. Irv was given the grand town, including the acreage and Naomi's two horses. Morrie was surprised that Naomi had invited Irv without first discussing it with him but made no mention of it. He was happy to see his old friend and was feeling some guilt

over ignoring him for so many months. After dinner
Naomi found a excuse to leave the two friends alone for a
while.

"So, Morrie how are you adjusting to country
living? It's quite a change from your busy private
practice in Philadelphia."

"It's taking me a while but I remain quite busy.
No worries about patients but the house still requires a
good bit of upkeep. Fortunately we have help with the
lawn…excuse me, pasture. We've made some friends
out here and I've joined the synagogue. Naomi is still
doing some school psych. I don't get into the city as
much as we once did."

"It's certainly peaceful out here. Reminds me of
my farm upstate and a lot closer. Are you doing any
professional work?"

"I've maintained my license but except for CE
credits I don't get to meetings much any more. I've

developed some other interests. Somehow psychology doesn't seem to have all the answers."

"What type of interests?"

"More religious, spiritual. I'm studying Hebrew, doing some theological explorations. Unlike you, religious feeling has come to me late in life."

"That can be a good thing. We all become more introspective as we grow older."

"Yes, that's exactly right. I feel I've ignored my sore spiritual needs most of my life. Trying to makeup for it now."

"How's your health?"

"All right for an old man. A little arthritis. Comes with the territory. We walk a couple of miles every day."

"So you're…what…67 now?"

"Yup. I've got a couple of years on you."

"Thinking about death…the afterlife?"

"I suppose so. Not more than is healthy. Are you doing a clinical assessment here?"

"Somewhat, I suppose so. Just concerned about you. Life changes are difficult at our age and you've made a pretty drastic change. Just wondering about how you are handling it?"

"Naomi put you up to this?"

"She's worried about you."

"I thought it was a little strange that she invited you without talking about it first. Not that I don't enjoy our talks."

"We haven't done this lately. I miss the camaraderie."

"Time passes quickly out here. We're an hour away now. I know that's just a rationalization I'll try and do better."

"Good. Me too. Now tell me what you're really into. Stop screwing around with me."

"Kabbalah. I'm reading the Torah and looking at hidden meanings."

"Numerology?"

"Yes."

"It's fringe area, even for Kabbalists. There were rabbis at Yeshiva when I studied there that believed. We looked at them as "meahuga." (crazy)

"Maybe it's not. I've had some bizarre experiences this past year."

"Of a religious nature?"

"More mystical than truly religious. You know I've had an interest in the mind-body problem for years. I've been writing a book titled "In search of the human mind. Haven't touched it lately. The neuroscientists have taken over the field and I'm no expert in fMRIs and such It's the soul I'm interested in. I'm a dualist. Plato was right, not Aristotle. The soul cannot be found in neuron firings. Psychology started out focused on subjective impressions, perception v. sensation. as you well know. Wundt, Weber, Fechner, psychophysics. That's what they were studying in a sense, but empirically not philosophically. That's how psychology split off from philosophy. Helmholtz led us away from the 18th century debates of Hume, Berkeley, and Kant."

"Yes, but the issues are no less relevant today. Einstein knew that."

"Oh so you've been studying relativity as well?"

'Not exactly but I've talked with the good professor."

"You've what?"

"At first I thought it was a dream but it seemed real. It wasn't the only occasion. Nor was he the only dead person I've encountered. I've had out-of-body experiences. And I've done time travel."

"Morrie, I can't believe what I am hearing. What about Kabbalah? What have you learned from the Torah?"

"You won't believe that either. I think that reincarnation is a distinct possibility. I believe that the soul survives after death.

"What evidence is there?"

"There are many recorded instances of apparitions appearing to people."

'You of all people understand about hallucinations."

"Irv. In your family what was done after a death—when the family sat "shiva.?"

"We covered the mirrors with sheets."

"Exactly. It was considered dangerous. You might lose your soul in the mirror, or the soul of the departed might be trapped in the glass."

"Superstition Morrie."

"I'm just showing you that people believe in disembodied souls."

"So you think you have been reincarnated?"

"I believe I am Moses."

"You are Morris Schwartz, Moshe in Hebrew."

"I believe I led my people out of Egypt across the red Sea."

The conversation continued for another hour. At around midnight a visibly shaken Irv Werlinski left for home."

30

Diagnosis

Schizophrenia is primarily a thinking disorder. It tends to run in families, although non-specific genetic link has been identified. The label is a waste basket category for many seemingly related conditions. There are three types of symptoms, termed positive, negative, and cognitive. Positive symptoms are hallucinations—hearing voices, seeing things that are not there. Delusions are false beliefs that are often bizarre.

They may include delusions of grandeur and feelings of persecution. There is a loss of contact with reality. Negative symptoms are difficulty in planning, speaking, expressing feelings, and finding pleasure in life. Cognitive symptoms are unusual thought processes, disorganized thinking, disorder language and use of strange words.

***

Professor Clifford Underweood, M.D., Fellow of

the American Psychoiatric Association, Chairman of the

Psychiatry Department of Jefferson Hospital, was

regarded by his residents as a pompous ass. No one

could faulty his credentials, his long list of publications in

prestigious psychiatric journals, or his position on the

Executive Committee of the APA. He was regarded as a

leading expert nationally on schizophrenia and had served

on the President's Committee on Mental health. For all

of that, he was an arrogant, opinionated, officious faculty

member and difficult to please. He conducted a weekly

seminar with residents who were obliged to present their

cases along with diagnostic formulations and treatment

plans. It was a formal meeting attended by all the

residents and ancillary staff as well former residents, now

in private practice and eager to remain on the good side

of Dr. Underwood and remain on his list of private

practicianers for referrals. It was to Dr. Underwood that

Naomi was referred by her family physician when she described Morrie's symptoms. Naomi researched his credentials and was impressed. Furthermore, Morrie had assured her that he had no prior professional contact with Dr. Underwood or Jefferson Hospital and would not be reluctant to see him.

Naomi was prepared for what Irv revealed to her. She had been concerned since Morrie revealed his visions to her and was less than comfortable with his preoccupation with Kabbalah. Irv believed Morrie was having a breakdown, likely schizophrenic. Irv, always somewhat intellectualized was sensitive to Naomi's concern about Morrie but retreated to an academic discussion of the symptoms. Morrie seemed to be having hallucinations as well as delusions of grandeur that suggested paranoia but there did not seem to be persecutory beliefs. Furthermore, Morrie had not lost his clinical insights and was well aware of the implications of his perceptions and beliefs. Nevertheless he insisted that, despite the bizarre nature of his visions and beliefs, he was not deranged.

Irv offered to speak with Morrie along with Naomi about a psychiatric referral. Naomi opted to handle it herself but to keep Irv informed.

**

Underwood assigned the initial history taking to Joe Pesche, one of his residents.

Joe spent about an hour with Morrie and Naomi, obtaining a brief history which he dictated at his desk immediately after the interview. He asked the department secretary to have it ready for Dr. Underwood within the hour. Morrie and Naomi were asked to remain in the waiting room during this time. Naomi was a little miffed; Morrie had expected as much.

Undrerwood glanced briefly at Pesche's summary. Pesche reminded him that Morrie was a retired psychologist who was demonstrating some bizarre behavior, concerning his wife and best friend. Morris had requested that in light of his professional status his material not be generally presented at staff meetings or seminars.

"So he wants special treatment?"

"Well, I can understand his concern. We owe him some professional courtesy."

"Yeah, yeah, OK. We'll keep it quiet. But this is a training hospital. Our seminars are important."

"He seems like a decent sort of fellow."

"I know the type."

Finally, Morrie and Naomi were shown into Underwood's consulting room. Pesche excused himself and left."

"So tell me why you are here, Dr. Schwartz."

"Mostly at my wife's insistence. She is concerned about me"

"Is there reason for her concern?"

"I can see why she is concerned. I have reassured her I am fine but she and my friend Irv are in agreement that I need help."

'You told Dr. Pesche that you have had some strange experiences."

"You might call them visions. Naomi thought they were dreams."

"What exactly did they consist of?"

"There were some out of body experiences and time travel. I spoke with some renowned people."

"Such as…"

"Spinoza, Maimonides, Einstein?"

"I'm not familiar with the second one."

"Maimonides was a Jewish philosopher…17 century. Somewhat mystic."

"Spinoza and Einstein were also Jewish, weren't they."

"Yes, and all were rebels against orthodoxy."

"And you, too are Jewish?

"I am Jewish but only recently have drawn closer to my heritage."

"Are you also a rebel?"

"I never considered myself as such."

"And what was the nature of your conversations with these great men?"

"I asked them about God, the meaning of life, the coming of the messiah. I didn't plan to encounter them. It just happened. I was confused by the experience."

"Did you get any answers?

"Yes, but it was only later that I realized there was a meaning to the experience.

That I was chosen for something."

"What led you to that conclusion?"

"It was a gradual awakening. I've always been a skeptic about religion and religious experiences. I was empirically trained...accept nothing without evidence."

"And now?"

"I'm not so sure. I've been told I am psychic ,clairvoyant."

"You are spending a great deal of time studying the bible, your wife tells us."

"The Torah—the first five books of the Old Testament."

"Your religion tells you that you are the chosen people, does it not?"

"It does. Chosen for persecution, oppression, extermination much of the time, it seems."

"And you now believe that you especially have been chosen for something/"

"I find some evidence for that."

"Empirical evidence?"

"Of course not. There are some things that go beyond empiricism."

"Just what is this…Kabbalah?"

"It is a way of communicating with God, becoming one with God."

"I have many Jewish friends. Young Dr. Pesche is Jewish. He doesn't talk with God."

"Have you asked him? Would he tell you if he was? Isn't prayer really talking with God?"

"Does God talk back to you?"

"God has many ways of communicating to us."

"Our job here, Dr. Schwartz, is to sort out religious faith from disturbed thinking."

"I spent a career trying to be a good diagnostician, among other things."

"So what is your diagnosis, Dr. Schwartz?"

"Aren't physicians trained not to treat themselves?"

"You're begging the question. If a patient presented with what you've told us, what would be your DSM diagnosis?"

"Hallucinations, delusions. Likely schizophrenia. Delusions of grandeur...paranoia."

"Aha, insight."

"Not so fast, Dr. Underwood. I don't accept it here."

"What is your evidence?

"No secondary or cognitive symptoms. I can examine my own reactions. No word salad. I don't appear strange or bizarre. I don't have any persecutory delusions."

"Your wife says you have been withdrawing more and more."

"My studies are time consuming."

"Is it worth it? You are jeopardizing your marriage."

"I need to work on that."

"What great insights have you arrived at from your studies?"

"My people have a long and great heritage. I am part of that heritage. I may in the past have placed a special role. I may still have a role to play."

"Do you think you are the Messiah?"

"He is yet to come."

"Whom do you think you are?

"Moshe."

***

The patient is a 67 year old retired psychologist. He is married with grown children. It is his second marriage as well as his wife's. He is a practicing Jew. He is experiencing hallucinations and delusional thinking, without secondary symptoms of schizophrenia. There has been a marked personality change with increasing withdrawal from social and professional life. He is reasonably bright with a superficial knowledge of psychopathology and personality dynamics. There is evidence of paranoid grandiosity. While he denies feelings of persecution, the holds a grudge against the injustices he feels have been perpetrated on the Jewish people. While he maintains a friendly, cooperative demeanor, there is an underlying anger and belligerence very close to the surface. I believe he is a potential danger to others should anyone challenge his belief system.

Dx: Schizophrenia, paranoid type.

Rx: Maximum security hospitalization with a course of Stelazine therapy,

5 mg, bid.

Clifford Underwood, M.D., FAPA

31

Bedlam

The doctors are in charge but there was no doubt

about who ran the ward. Mollie

Peterson, Chief Nurse, made the important decisions.

Morris realized where the power lay within minutes after

being escorted to the Psychiatric Wing. He'd had enough

experience working with hospitals to be able to operate as

a patient. Needless to say it was not as Morris Schwartz,

Ph.D., who treated patients, participated in staffings,

made recommendations, but as Morrie, the new patient,

stripped of possessions, power, dignity and with the

additional stigma of paranoid schizophrenic. He wore no

label with that diagnosis but it might as well have been

stamped on his forehead. His chart was in the nurse's

room, open to inspection by every staff member. One

positive was that he was not placed in a hospital gown but

allowed to wear comfortable street clothes. He was

stripped of all but a few personal toilet articles, changes

of clothing and a book he had brought with him. Naomi

had taken his wallet, wrist watch, and left him with only a

few dollars for canteen items.

Morrie inventoried the cast of characters

comprising this personal drama. The metaphor was

accurate since it reflected his perception of what was

happening to him. He had agreed to go along with the

hospitalization. It would relieve Naomi's fears for his

safety and give him a chance to assess what was going on

internally. He wasn't happy with the medication but if

that was what he had to do to move on, so be it.

Nevertheless, there was an unreal quality to his situation.

He was not oblivious to the paradox here. He was

hospitalized--under lock and key—because he had

allegedly lost contact with reality.

Yet, it was the setting they had immersed him into that

bore no resemblance to the real world. He took heart in

the belief that he was strong enough to maintain his identity despite how outrageous the external circumstance. Somehow he knew that he, too, would survive this cuckoo's nest.

Mollie reported to the ward doctor that first day that the new patient was polite, cooperative, neat and clean, unlike most of her admissions. He did not appear to match his diagnosis, despite his history of delusions. In fact, he seemed to be mildly amused by his hospitalization. He took in everything around him, asked intelligent questions, and seemed more like staff than patient. Her medical superior cautioned her about making snap judgments.

"It's not unusual for paranoids to have a smug, supercilious attitude. It's part of their grandiosity. They see themselves as above all this, as being falsely accused, smarter than those who are treating him. Give it a while.

He's show his true nature soon enough. His hostility is only thinly sealed over."

"I suppose so," Mollie, admitted "but he seems more humble than arrogant. I hope he can cope with the other characters in here."

Morrie circled the day room , stopping to introduce himself to the others, one by one. His diagnostic skills had not left him. Joe in the corner was obviously depressed. He avoided the others, avoided eye contact. The circles under his eyes announced his sleeplessness. He stared hopelessly at Morrie, unable to fathom his cheerful greeting or even to respond. Morrie patted him on the shoulder and assured him that things would improve. Morrie learned later that Joe was also a new admission. He had made a suicide attempt with pills after his wife left him with the children.

Burton was loud, talkative, excessively exuberant. He paced the room, offered to do odd jobs, moved furniture around, did push-ups, organized games of pinochle. Hypomanic, Morrie speculated.

Fred was the ward bully, pugnacious, challenging, threatening. He had his group of followers whom he ruled by intimidation. He had the physique of a boxer and he threw his weight around accordingly. Fred didn't wait for Morris to approach him. He challenged him shortly after Morris arrived on the ward, demanding cigarettes. Morrie assured him that he didn't smoke but that if any cigarettes came his way he'd be happy to share. Fred grudgingly backed off. Morrie tagged him paranoid, then winced with the realization that he was being equated with this patient. Morrie realized that he would constitute to threaten Fred, who would know his diagnosis. He would have o watch his back. Morrie was not surprised that, despite the effect of psychotropic medications, it was still possible to make diagnoses from clinical observation. He made a mental note to observe how different diagnoses interacted with each other, perhaps keep notes for a paper "The psychologist turned patient." "Oh, sure," he thought. "All Fred has to do is find me taking notes about his behavior."

***

Morrie took his place on the morning medicine line. Patients lined up at the nurses's station and were dispensed their medications under the eye of an attendant. The patient was obliged to swallow the pill before moving away from the window. Attendents were wise to the maneuvers of those who would try to "cheek" the medicine without swallowing it, disposing of in the trash after moving from the window. Liquids, of course, were more difficult to fake. Morrie had no intention of faking the pill but he wanted to know it's side effects. He asked the nurse for a print- out of the drug properties, company. The nurse told him it was not something he needed to know at this time. Rather than make a fuss he called Naomi and asked her to check out the PDR and let

him know what he might expect.

Morrie had a superficial working knowledge of drug

actions so there were no surprises   when he read the pages

Naomi had printed from the Internet. He knew that Stelazine

was   used for treating the thinking and perceptual disruptions

of schizophrenia. He knew that   strong psychotropic

medica5tions over time might cause tardive dyskenesia, a

condition   producing involuntary, and sometimes, permanent

twitches in the face and body. These problems were more

frequent in older patients. This was a concern but he knew that

tardive dyskinesia occurred after prolonged exposure or after

sudden cessation of the   drugs. Morrie might look forward

to allergic reactions, anemia, blurred vision, blood

problems…The list went on and Morrie stopped reading.

His curiosity about what the   medication would do to his visions

and out-of-body experiences might be interesting. He

regretted that in the past he had referred patients too

callously for psychotropic medication without considering the possible consequences.

***

Morrie had been in the hospital about a week without any apparent changes in his thinking or perceptions that he could identify. He was already considering a request for discharge. He knew the nurses were watching him closely and looking for signs of disturbance. He treated them politely, joking with them when appropriate. He knew he had provided no ammunition for justifying lock-up in a closed wing. Even the diagnosis must be in question, he reasoned.

The ward physician interviewed him every few days and asked about seeing or hearing things. Morrie answered honestly that he had not experienced anything unusual. Even Dr, Underwood, who made rounds occasionally, seemed to be puzzled. Morrie had not abandoned any of the ideas he knew they labeled as delusional. No one asked him about these beliefs and Morrie certainly wasn't going to volunteer anything. He took comfort in the thought that the hospitalization was unnecessary and even the Stelazine had no visible effect. It did not occur to him that the staff were attributing his normal appearing behavior as a response to medication, rather than the absence of pre-drug pathology, which they did not challenge.

Although Morrie had a private bathroom attached to his room, he used the :head' in the day room rather than walk back to his room. Morrie entered the lavatory as usual on the Monday a week after his admission. He had grown accustomed to the uneventful war routine and was not anticipating trouble.

Fred had Joe pinned against the wall. Joc's pants were down at his ankles. Fred was humping him from the rear. Joe was crying silently and offering no resistance. Morrie yelled for the attendants and began pulling Fred away from Joe. When help arrived Morrie

was between the two of them with Joe's back to him.

Before Morris could speak Fred began shouting. This

new guy was raping Joe. I tried to   pull them apart. Joe

offered no denial of that account. The guard asked Joe if that

was   what had happened. Joe shook his head yes, silently.

ewas infuriated. The two aides strong armed him to a

locked isolation room. The ward physician wrote an order for a

24 hour "time out." The room was devoid of furniture and

padded. A soiled mattress was on the floor. There was no

bathroom. Morrie had to request permission to be escorted to the

bathroom and was observed while using the facilities. The door

to the room had a small window. Patients in isolation had to be

observed every 15 minutes and the time recorded.

The incident was relayed to Dr. Underwood.

"I was wondering when the honeymoon period would end

with Dr. Morris, Ph.D. Homosexual acting out is common in

paranoids. Freud werote about it. The dynamics are simple.

The patient feels "I love you" toward a liked-sexed person. He is threatened by the thought and it is transformed to 'I hate you.' by the defense of reaction formation. That too is threatening and the thought is projected outward as 'He hates me.' Hence, the paranoia. Nevertheless the homosexual feelings may break through. I knew there was underlying hostility in that pseudohealer."

"He claims he walked in on Fred doing Joe."

"They're both paranoid. Probably they were fighting over their bitch. Joe fingered Schwartz. Let him stay in isolation another few days."

Morrie had now been initiated into the culture of the psychiatric hospital. Never again would he fail to sympathize with hospitalized mental patients.

32

Moving On

Morie never did serve the rest of his isolation sentence. When Naomi learned of his circumstances she moved him from the hospital to a small proprietary hospital in Northeast Philadelphia. Morrie's stay at Oxford Psychiatric was not fully covered by insurance and quite expensive but more pleasant and short-lived. The staff re-addressed his diagnosis of paranoia. Demonstrating no aberrant behavior, he seemed a model patient and was weaned off the Stelazine and soon discharged. He agreed to begin outpatient therapy, which he did for about six months He continued to study Kabbalah and to attend Sabbath services at his synagogue.

It is unclear whether he continued to experience visions and harbor ideas of his own historic significance. If he did it remained a personal affair that he shared with no one. His marriage remained strong. Morrie continued to work on his book, Search for the Human Mind

But changed the title to Search for the Human Soul: Odyssey of

a Psychologist. The book was never published but epaid for a

private printing of fifty copies which he instructed to be

distributed to his children, grandchildren, and any close friends

whom Naomi believed might be interested.

Morrie had only one more spiritual voyage. He found

himself in his own room which looked strangely older. The

furniture had frayed, there was more clutter, and there were

objects he did not presently own. A desk calendar lay open to an

August day, 2010. Once aware of what he was seeing, he was

not surprised to see an older, more feeble version of himself

enter the room and sit down at the desk. The apparition, if that's

what it was, was completely gray and had walked in with a cane.

The older man addressed his former self:

"Nu Morrie, you see what you have become?"

"There are no surprises."

"What have I yet to learn? What can you teach me?"

"Stop obsessing. Stop trying to prove yourself. You're a good man. You've done fine.

Enjoy your last few years."

"And you are happy now?"

"I am. I haven't much longer. I've accomplished enough. I can go in peace."

'My visions. Were they real?"

"Give it up, boychick. It's not for you to know."

"Our mother talked of her approaching death as her "great reward." Will it be that?

"We will soon find out. Rest in peace can apply equally before death."

"Will I see you again?"

"Are you seeing me now?"

***

Morrie continues to live in the country. After his hospital stay he decided to return to private practice. In 2005, Morrie won a large sum of money with a five dollar ticket in the

Pennsylvania lottery. Two years later he distributed his book to family and friends. Morrie had shared it with Naomi before the printing and she understood why he decided to keep it secret so long. He had intended to withhold distribution of the book until after his death. But as he aged his vanity and conceits faded and he was less concerned about what others would make of his paranormal experiences. And so his children learned of a side of their father they had never encountered.

The book documented Morrie's childhood years, his college days and graduate training, his army experience, and private practice. A final chapter of the book described a series of unusual experiences and explorations into the occult. He explained his obsession with understanding the nature of the human soul and the possibility of life after death. He justified his efforts to find answers in the Torah and it's hidden meanings. But it was not Kabbalah that eventually afforded Morris the answers he was seeking. Rather, he attributed his new found serenity to a small book by European psychiatrist Victor Frankel, a Holocaust survivor of Auschwitz and Dachau. Frankel rejected the psychoanalytic thinking of the day attributing neuroses to conflicts among the instincts. Rather he accepted an existential belief in the necessity for finding meaning in one's life, even in suffering. Morrie ended his epic with the following paragraphs:

"My conversion to existential philosophy and psychology came late in life. Psychologists have been chasing a false God in trying to help people achieve happiness and reduce anxiety, guilt, and behavioral symptoms. Frankel, exposed to the most heinous dehumanization inflicted on a people in history found meaning in his experiences and advised others to find meaning in their own lives, no matter how unbearable the circumstances. Life's purpose is personal and cannot be provided by professional healers.

I came to the realization that my psychic experiences, my beliefs in my own historical and religious significance had such meaning. For many years I had been asking the wrong questions.

Was there an immaterial mind or soul? Was there the possibility

of life after death?

Were out-of-body experiences and time travel possible? Was I

really having paranormal experiences or was I, indeed, psychotic

and delusional? These questions pale in the face of what was

staring me in the face all along. Why was I having these

experiences? If life has meaning, as most philosophers and my

alter egos—Maimonides, Spinoza, Einstein, and Freud – led me

to believe, then these excursions of my soul also have meaning.

Were they real or illusions? It does not matter. They were real

to me. They sent me in certain directions. They led me to

challenge my psychological discipline, to return to my religion,

to recognize my heritage, to acknowledge my predecessors, to be

concerned about the hereafter, and my destiny. They led me to go

beyond my own life and to leave something to my descendants,

which is, after all, the purpose of this book. So if I have

something to offer those who come after me it is to open yourself

to whatever you encounter, without being blinded by dogma,

prejudice, and blind conformity to what is considered acceptable, scientific, and unassailable."

***

A trillion light years away a shimmering star made transit along a pre-determined route, unnoticed and unexplained.